# Just Plain Bob

## 9 STORIES IN 1

# HOT and TIGHT

## EROTICA SHORT STORIES, VOL. 21

# WARNING

This book contains sexually explicit scenes and adult language. It may be considered offensive to some readers. This book is for sale to adults ONLY.

Please store your files wisely where they cannot be accessed by underage readers.

\* \* \* \* \* \* \* \* \* \* \* \* \* \* \* \* \* \*

## WANT FREE COPIES OF MY BOOKS?
Just visit my blog and download free copies of my books:
**awesomeauthors.org/justplainbob**

## About the Publisher

**4Fun Publishing,** a member of **BLVNP Incorporated**, 340 S. Lemon #6200, Walnut CA 91789, info@blvnp.com / legal@blvnp.com
NOTE: Due to the highly emotional reaction of some people to works of erotic fiction, any email sent to the above address that contains foul language or religious references is automatically deleted by our anti-spam software and will not be seen. All other communications are welcome.

## DISCLAIMER

Please don't be stupid and kill yourself. This book is a work of FICTION. Do not try any new sexual practice that you find in this book. It is fiction and not to be confused with reality. Neither the author nor the publisher or its associates assume any responsibility for any loss, injury, death or legal consequences resulting from acting on the contents in this book. Every character in this book is over 18 years of age. The author's opinions are not to be construed as the opinions of the publisher. The material in this book is for entertainment purposes ONLY. Enjoy.

Erotica Short Stories, Vol. 21
# Hot & Tight
### 9 Stories in 1

By: Just Plain Bob

© **Just Plain Bob 2015**
ISBN: 978-1-68030-363-6

# Asshole

It has taken me years to learn to accept my lot in life. I've been called an asshole ever since junior high and I used to take great exception to it. More than a few fights came of it, but as I grew older I learned that it was stupid to get into a fight with someone just because he made a true statement. I am an asshole. How big an asshole you ask? Well, how big of an asshole is someone who seduces his brother's wife less than a month after the wedding ceremony? How big of an asshole are you if you start fucking the woman your dad is going to marry a good two months before they take their vows? That's how big of an asshole I am.

Fucking Mary and Elise wasn't something that just happened, I wanted both of them and I set out to get them. I figured Mary would be the hardest, her being an older woman embarking on her second marriage, wise in the ways of the world. Boy, was I ever wrong! I am still not sure whether I got her or she got me. Not that it matters. The bottom line is that we both are getting what we want, and on a regular basis. Getting Elise wasn't much harder and I'm happy to be able to say that both were worth whatever effort that it took.

\*\*\*

Dad brought Mary home to meet the family and have dinner with us one night. I wanted her the moment I saw her and the fact that she was eighteen years older did not mean a damn thing to me. After that first night Mary became a regular visitor to our house and eventually she moved in and began living with dad. One night we were in the kitchen together - she was drying dishes and I was sitting at the table, sipping coffee and watching her. She turned toward me and asked:

"Why are you looking at me like that?"

I smiled at her, "If you have to ask the question you wouldn't understand the answer."

She cocked her head to one side and smiled, "I'm going to have to be careful around you, aren't I?"

"Not too careful I hope," I replied.

She stared at me silently for a few moments and then turned back to the dishes. In that moment the dynamics between us had changed. It was two days before I saw Mary again and I caught her glancing my way several times during the course of the evening. We both knew what I wanted and the looks she gave me seemed to say:

"Thank you for the interest. I'm flattered, but forget it."

The day my dad announced that he and Mary were going to get married my brother George and I threw a party for them. I caught Mary alone in the kitchen after she'd had several drinks and was in a mellow mood. She smiled at me and asked:

"Are you going to mind having me around all the time now?"

"Not a chance," I said, "The more you're around, the more opportunities I'll have, and sooner or later I'll get what I want."

Mary laughed, "You can't be serious!"

I took both of her hands and placed them on my hard cock. "Does this feel serious enough for you?"

I expected her to pull away and slap my face, but she surprised me by squeezing my dick. I leaned forward and kissed her on the mouth and she surprised me again by slipping me a little tongue. She gave my dick another squeeze and stepped back.

"You are such an asshole. I can't believe that you would treat your own father's future wife like this," and she left the room.

Our next encounter took place following a party that my Uncle Bob threw for the happy couple. We'd all been drinking and having a good time and all of us were in a pretty good mood. Near the end of the party my dad came up to me and asked me if I would see to it that Mary got home since he had a few things that he needed to go do.

On the way I detoured to a spot that was the local 'lovers' lane'. Mary asked me why I'd stopped there and I said:

"This is where people go to make out."

I pulled her to me and kissed her and she responded. For about five minutes we made out like teenagers and then I unzipped, took out my dick and placed her hand on it. She pulled her hand away, but did not break the kiss. It took two more tries before she left her hand on my cock and slowly started to stroke it. For several minutes she jacked me and soon I could feel myself getting ready to let go.

"Let's get in the back seat," I said and Mary shook her head 'no'.

"This is all you get from me and for the life of me I can't figure out why I'm even giving you this much."

Just then I spit a huge load of cum out of the head of my cock and it went all over the place. Mary laughed, "It's a good thing I wasn't giving you a blowjob - that might have taken the back of my head off."

We drove the rest of the way home in silence. When I pulled into the driveway and shut off the engine, Mary reached for her door handle.

"Don't I at least get a goodnight kiss?"

She hesitated and then she leaned toward me offering me her mouth. My mouth touched hers and just as before she slipped me some tongue. I responded, and then we were at it like teenagers again. After several minutes of furious necking I pulled free:

"You know," I said, "that I'm not letting you out of this car until I've fucked you."

She started for the door, but I grabbed her.

"You are not strong enough to get away from me and the more you struggle the more commotion it will cause. Sooner or later someone will come out to see what all the fuss is about and when that happens you are going to have to explain all the cum stains on your dress. It won't matter what you say, it will be your word against mine and those cum stains will be pretty damning evidence."

All the fight went out of her.

"All right," she said, "Let's get it over with" and she leaned back against the door.

"No," I said, "I'm not going to let you just lay there like a log. I want some of the passion you showed when we were necking" and I pulled her to me.

It took longer this time, a lot longer, but eventually she had her tongue half way down my throat. Another five minutes and I had her bra off and only moments after that my fingers were in her pussy. She pulled her mouth from mine,

"We can't do this" she said, "It just isn't right."

"Sure we can," I said, and we did. Once in the back seat of the car and twice in her bed when we got into the house. There could have been a third time, but we were both afraid that dad would be home soon.

\*\*\*

For the next week Mary and I fucked like rabbits whenever we found ourselves alone. And then one night I came home to find her washing vegetables in the kitchen sink. My brother was the only one home and he was upstairs taking a shower. I walked up behind her and pinned her against the sink. I pulled up her skirt, pushed down her panties, bent her forward over the sink and started to work my cock toward her cunt. She resisted at first, but I had her pinned pretty good. Suddenly she relaxed, moved her feet apart to give me better access, my cock found the target and I began to push into her.

"Why are you doing this to me?" she said.

"Because I can. And because you have the hottest, tightest cunt I have ever been in."

I fucked her hard for several minutes and during that time she had at least one orgasm. We were so engrossed in what we were doing that we did not hear the shower stop. It wasn't until I saw movement out of the corner of my eye and glanced in its direction that I knew my brother was standing in the doorway watching. I was almost ready to cum so I motioned him to come closer. He immediately knew what I had in mind and he moved toward us as silent as a creeping cat. When I came I pushed hard into Mary and emptied myself in her pussy and then, instead of just staying and letting my cock drain as I usually did, I took one quick step back and George stepped forward and took my place. His hard cock slid right into Mary's well-lubricated pussy and he began to fuck her with hard, steady strokes. So quick was the change that it hadn't yet registered with Mary. In fact, the first she was aware of the fact that it wasn't me fucking her was when she saw me standing off to the side using dad's camcorder. She was barely able to muster a "You bastard" as she experienced another orgasm.

"You know you love it," I said and kept filming. "Besides, every family album needs photos showing what a loving family they are."

Half an hour later, while Mary was sucking George's cock and I was fucking her from behind George asked me when dad was due home.

"His flight gets in at three," I said.

"Great!" said George. "That means we've got her all night."

I laughed, "Yeah Bro, we've got her all night."

From that night on whenever dad was out of town either George, or me and quite often both of us, spent the night in Mary's bed. She always resisted at first, but then she always gave in. We even fucked her on her wedding day - two hours before the ceremony we were double-teaming her.

*** 

Since she and dad returned from their honeymoon not one week goes by that either George or I get a taste of Mary. I decided that I needed to move out and get my own place and George met and fell in love with a very foxy lady and he moved out too.

Funny thing though, given how she always resisted us, you would have thought she would be glad to see us move out of the house and get our own places. But every time, and I do mean every time, that dad went out of town Mary would call us to come help her do something - move furniture, unclog a drain, or replace a blown fuse. And every time, and again I do mean every time, we would go and we end up in bed with Mary. In fact, George spends so much time in Mary's bed that he leaves an opening in his own and I just couldn't bear the thought of the lovely Elise having that empty space beside her, but that's another story.

*** 

Compared to Mary (who really wasn't all that hard) getting to Elise was a piece of cake. About three weeks after my brother George married Elise, he had to go out of town on business. He asked me to look in on her from time to time to make sure she was all right and to do whatever I could for her if she needed help.

The first day he was gone I called Elise and asked her to have dinner with me ("I know how lonely you must be this being your first separation, yadda, yadda, yadda) and she agreed. I took her to a place where they had good food and a dance band. I kept her wineglass full all through dinner and by the time we had finished eating she had quite a buzz on. She readily agreed when I asked her if she would like to stay awhile for some dancing and I ushered her to a table in a fairly dark corner of the club. Elise started drinking vodka tonics and every time she would get up to go to the ladies room I'd get her another double.

There were a few other people there that we knew and I invited them over to join us, but by ten o'clock they had all left except for Gary and Frank. Also by then Elise was a very happy drunk. She was on the dance floor with Gary and I had just ordered her another double when Frank said to me:

"If it works let me know. I've always wanted some of that."

I gave him a big grin. It was around eleven-thirty and I was dancing a nice slow one with Elise. I figured it was time to make my move so I pulled her close and pressed my stiff cock into her and held it there.

She giggled, "Naughty boy. You shouldn't do that. All you boys are being naughty tonight."

"They just like you Elise," I told her.

She giggled again, "I know what they like and they are just being nice to me because I've got one."

I smiled to myself and thought, "Time to go!" We finished the dance and went back to our table. I ordered another round 'for the road', a double for Elise, of course, as she made one last trip to the ladies room. Frank looked at me:

"Don't forget, okay?"

I had a particularly evil thought, "Give me a number where I can reach you in a hurry" and Frank wrote down his cell phone number for me.

*** 

On the way to her house Elise giggled and talked the way silly drunks do.

"All the boys were naughty tonight. They kept poking me with their thingys. That was a naughty thing to do, wasn't it? Why were they so naughty? They shouldn't be naughty, should they?"

I told her that it was all her fault, "If you weren't so sexy their thingys wouldn't get stiff."

She reached over and put her hand on my crotch. "Oops! That was naughty of me wasn't it? Your thingy isn't hard." She pouted, "You don't think I'm sexy? I thought you were my friend - I thought you liked me."

This is as good a time as any I thought, and I unzipped myself and brought out my hard cock. I took Elise's hand and put it on my stiff dick, "Still think I don't like you?"

She giggled, "Bad boy. Naughty, naughty bad boy" but her hand stayed on my dick. She giggled some more, "But I guess I'm being naughty too."

The first time was on the living room couch. I undressed her and then myself and just as I was getting ready to push into her she giggled again, "I don't think I'm supposed to do this now that I'm married. I don't...oops" she giggled as I drove home, "Too late."

The second time was in her bed and when I'd gotten my rocks off

I picked up the bedside phone and called Frank. "Get over here and give me some help. The front door is open. We are in the bedroom, just come on up."

Elise hadn't even noticed me on the phone. She lay on the bed giggling and dragging her fingers along her cunt lips and then she would hold them up and look at the cum on them and giggle, "I'm a bad girl - I've been a very, very bad girl" and I said to myself, "And baby, you ain't through yet!"

Twenty minutes later as I was stuffing Elise's 'brown eye' Frank came into the room followed by Gary. Frank said, "He's always wanted a taste of her too so I brought him along."

While the two of them undressed I concentrated on pumping my load into her ass and when I had cum I got out of the way and let Frank take my place. Elise didn't even notice - she had her eyes closed and was moaning (thank God the giggling had stopped) "I'm a bad girl. I'm being bad. Naughty, naughty me."

I left the room and went looking for George's video camera. I found it and grabbed one of his tapes (only fair, right? His wife, his bed, his camera, his tape - had a kind of symmetry to it). When I got back to the bedroom Gary was kneeling in front of Elise holding the back of her head while he fucked her face. Frank was still plowing her ass:

"I can't believe how tight she is, even after you were there. Your brother must not use it."

For the next hour I taped Elise, Frank and Gary as they worked their way through various positions and couplings. My favorite was when Frank fucked her pussy while Gary fucked her ass. I didn't fuck Elise any more that night, not because I didn't want to, but because if I did either Gary or Frank might have picked up the camera and filmed it. If this tape ever surfaced I did not want to be seen on it.

When Frank and Gary had worn themselves out and left I took

the camcorder and zoomed in on Elise's face - she looked dazed and then she smiled and blew a kiss into the camera. I panned down the length of her body, rolled her over and got a shot of her gaping asshole with all of the cum running out of it. Then I went home and slept like a baby.

The next day I went over to see Elise. She had a murderous look on her face when she came to the door, "You bastard! You lousy rotten bastard."

"Hold on," I said, "Is that anyway to talk to the man who's going to make you a star? The man who will make your name a household word?"

She looked at me, "What are you talking about?" I walked past her into the living room, put the tape in the VCR, turned on the TV and hit the 'play' button. And then we watched as Elise, Gary and Frank filled the screen. Elise, a stunned look on her face, dropped heavily onto the couch and I joined her there, We watched the tape in silence and when I felt the moment was right I exposed myself and took her hand and placed it on my cock. She didn't pull it away, instead she asked, "What is it you want?"

"Simple" I said, "I just want you to fuck me anytime I want. Me, and maybe a few of my friends."

I put a hand on the back of her head and pushed it down. Just before her lips closed on my dick she said, "God! You are such a fucking asshole!"

I smiled, "Yes! I know!"

# End of the 1$^{st}$ Story

# Fred's Whore

"You know your choices Bess. Stop your whining and get ready to do it or get your ass out of here." My wife Bess gave me a nasty look, but then she turned and went upstairs to get ready for the evening.

My marriage to Bess was pretty much a sham, but it hadn't always been that way. For almost ten years it had been what I would have called a model marriage and indeed people had pointed at us and said, "That's what a marriage should be like." Not anymore! Six months ago the wheels had come off and the marriage had cratered. That Bess and I are still together is because Bess won't give up on trying to win me back. I don't think it is possible, but if she wants to try I'll let her. There is a price that she has to pay for being able to stay with me while she tries work things out with me and she's not happy that she has to pay it, but pay it she does.

It all started when Bess and my brother's wife Ann went to a bachelorette party for my cousin Myra. Bess likes to sip the sauce so I expected her to come home smashed, but I wasn't worried because Ann doesn't drink and she would act as the designated driver. I also expected that she would come home late so I didn't wait up for her. I woke up at four in the morning needing to go to the bathroom and I noticed that Bess wasn't in the bed with me. I took my whiz and then checked the living room couch and then the rest of the house, but Bess wasn't there. I wasn't too worried because I knew she was with Ann.

I got up at my regular time at seven and still no Bess. I made coffee, took my shower, got dressed and at eight o'clock I called my brother's house. He answered and I asked him if Ann was there and he said she was and I asked him to have her come to the phone. There was a long pause and in the background I heard Ann say:

"I don't want to talk to him" and then my brother say, "You have to talk to him. It's not your fault and he'll know that."

When Ann came to the phone I told her that Bess wasn't at home, "She was riding with you Ann, what's going on?"

Ann hemmed and hawed and finally said, "I don't know what to tell you Fred."

"Well at least tell me if I should be calling the cops."

"I don't know Fred, I don't think so, but I really don't know."

"What's going on Ann? What is it you're not telling me?"

There was hesitation on her end of the line and I said, "Tell me now on the phone Ann or I'm coming over there and I will sit on your couch and stare at you until you tell me in person."

There were several seconds of silence and then the story poured out of her.

The girls had been having a good time and Bess was drinking like she always did. One of the girls had hired some entertainment in the form of three - not one, but three - male strippers and things had gotten pretty raunchy when the three of them had done their routines. The strippers were invited to stay and party and they did. There were several single girls there and they pretty much went after the strippers and a couple of the married women felt that wasn't fair and they started a friendly competition. Bess wasn't taking part in the competition, but Bess is an extremely sexy looking lady so even though she showed no interest in the strippers they showed an interest in her.

Ann had noticed the three men feeding Bess booze and she thought it was funny. "They thought they were going to hustle Bess; they didn't know that I was keeping an eye on her and that I would be the one she left with."

When Ann decided that it was time to go she decided that she should hit the restroom first before getting in the car to drive home. She was third in line to use the facilities and when she was done she went looking for Bess. When she couldn't find her she asked if anyone had seen her and one of the girls said she thought that Bess had stepped outside for some fresh air. Ann went outside just in time to see the three strippers hustle Bess into a car. Ann ran back in the house to get her purse and car keys, ran back outside, got in her car and tried to follow them, but got caught at a light and lost them.

"You're saying that somewhere three guys have Bess?"

Ann was silent for a couple of seconds and then she said "yes."

"And you don't think I should call the cops?"

"I didn't say that Fred. What I said was that I didn't know, but I didn't think so."

"How do you figure that?"

"Because Fred, everyone saw Bess leave with them. If anything bad happened to Bess all that you would have to do is tell the cops what agency they worked for and the cops would have them in no time and those guys know it. No, we both know what happened Fred and the cops can't do anything now that it's done unless Bess cries rape. As drunk as she was the rape charge would never stick. All the three guys would have to do is say Bess consented and Bess wouldn't honestly be able to remember if she had said yes or not. She'll call Fred, you just have to wait for it. She didn't know what she was doing Fred. Whatever happened she didn't know and she had no control. I'm sorry Fred, I really and truly am, but it wasn't my fault and it really wasn't hers either."

As I hung up the phone all I could think about was what the three guys had done or were doing to Bess. They'd had her all night and for all I knew they still had her. Three guys gangbanging my wife all night long and maybe all day long too.

The more I thought about it the madder I got and I called Ann again and asked her who had hired the strippers. She gave me the name and I called Shirley and found out whom she had hired the strippers from. Then I called The Fantasy Agency and asked to speak to the owner. He wasn't in so I was put through to the day manager. I told him that I wanted the names and addresses of the three men who had worked Myra's party and he refused to give them to me. Then I told him what had happened and told him he either give me the names or he could give them to the police and that I would make damn sure that a newspaper reporter would just happen to be in the neighborhood when the cops arrived. He told me he would call the owner and get back to me. I told him he had one hour and then I was going to the cops. He called me back in twenty minutes and gave me the information and then he told me that the three didn't work for the agency anymore as of the time of his conversation with his boss.

Before I could do anything with the information the phone rang and it was Ann. "Bess just called me. She's in a motel on the other side of town and she wants me to come and pick her up."

"Why didn't she call me?"

"She's afraid to. She was alone when she woke up, but could tell what had happened to her. She's afraid to face you."

"Tell me where it is, I'll go and get her."

"No Fred, let me do it. I'll give her a shoulder to cry on and try to ease her mind about having to face you."

"Ann, if the story you told me is true she doesn't have to worry about me."

"You and I know that Fred, she doesn't."

Bess spent three days crying and begging me for forgiveness and I must have told her fifty times that I did. Eventually she accepted my assertions that I forgave her and that I wanted to forget that it ever happened. I couldn't of course, there was no way I could ever forget that my wife had been gangbanged, but I had to try and convince her that I had. I was affectionate and loving and I tried to show that nothing had changed between us, but things had.

Before Bess had her 'lost night' we had enjoyed a rather robust sex life - five and sometimes six nights a week. Suddenly we were down to one or maybe two and only then if I refused to take no for an answer. I told myself it was natural for her to want to avoid sex for a while after what had happened to her and I thought that after a time things would go back to normal.

\*\*\*

Three months went by and things didn't get any better and I suggested that maybe we needed to seek some professional help. Bess told me that there wasn't any way she was going to see a shrink and that nothing was wrong with her. I was right on the edge of insisting when something happened that changed everything. I had gone for almost a month without sex and I was feeling extremely horny. I came home from work early one day and I pulled into the drive just as Bess was getting out of her car. She was wearing a short skirt and high heels and her long legs looked magnificent. I got an immediate hard on and when she opened the trunk of her car and bent forward to get some shopping bags out of the trunk I wanted to walk up behind her and take her from behind right then and there.

I helped her carry her bags into the house and when we had put them down I swept her up in my arms and headed for the bedroom.

"What are you doing Fred?"

"I'm going to ravish you my dear."

"No Fred, put me down. I don't want to."

"You never want to anymore Bess, but I do and tonight the drought ends."

"Damn it Fred, I said no! Now put me down."

I put her down - right on the bed - and then because she was determined to fight me off I decided not to waste any more time.

"I've put up with this shit ever since your night out with the boys and I've just decided that I'm not putting up with it any more. You are either going to be a wife to me Bess or you can go and find yourself a divorce lawyer."

And then I pushed the crotch band of her panties aside and pushed my hard cock into her. I slid right in and immediately realized that Bess had been freshly fucked. There is no sensation quite like that of sliding your cock into a pussy full of cum and once you have done it you never forget the feeling. In college I had taken part in a gangbang or three and I was well acquainted with what my cock was experiencing at that moment. I tried to keep my face neutral as I fucked Bess and looked down into her blazing eyes. Was this why she had not been having sex with me? To hide the fact that she was fucking someone else? I didn't know, but I was damned sure going to find out.

When it was over Bess said, "I can't believe that you just raped me."

"Yeah? Well you heard what I said. Either get back to being a wife to me or get yourself a lawyer and end the marriage. You won't let me get you professional help and I'm through waiting for you to get back to being your old self. It's your choice, at least for now."

"What does that mean?"

"It means that it is your choice now but that if you don't hurry up and make it maybe I'll be the one making the choice."

***

The next day I hired a private detective. He followed Bess for a week and that was long enough. He had pictures, he had names and addresses and he had places, times and dates. I paid him off and started going through his report. The names and addresses jogged my memory and I went looking for the list I had made when I had called The Fantasy Agency. Bess was cheating on me with the three assholes that had taken her away from Myra's party. I didn't waste any of my time wondering how much of Ann's and Bess's story of that night was true and how much of it was bullshit. The fact was that Bess was willingly seeing those three almost every day of the week. Sometimes only one of them, sometimes all three, but not her husband, oh no, God forbid she should take care of him.

It took me a week to learn what I needed to know and then to set things up and then things started to happen. At 9:15 on Thursday night James Weeks heard his car alarm go off. He looked outside of his apartment and saw the glow of a fire underneath his car. He came running down the steps from his second floor apartment and as he stepped off the bottom step he felt a blinding pain as a baseball bat crushed his right knee and as he fell to the ground the same thing happened to his left knee. Forty minutes later and eleven miles away the same thing happened to Steve Goddard. At 11:35 that same evening Jason Demming stepped out into the alley behind Angelina's Restaurant for his smoke break. When Jose Gonzales came out to dump the trash at 12:10 he found Jason rolling in pain on the ground with two smashed knees.

For the next two days I carefully watched Bess and I could tell she was nervous and upset about something, but even knowing what caused it I stayed quiet and just watched. Then I took a day off work and followed Bess. Her first stop was at St. Anthony's Hospital which was where they had Demming. Next she went to County General where Weeks and Goddard were occupying beds. I headed home, stopping at a florist to send flowers to all three men in Bess's name on the card. The next day I took half a day off work and was sitting at the kitchen table when Bess came home. She knew - she knew as soon as she visited and saw the flowers with her name on the card, and she knew as soon as she saw me sitting and waiting for her.

She stood there and stared at me for almost a minute and I just sat there and looked back at her. Finally she said, "Why?"

"Just my way of letting you know how upset I was when I found out that you wouldn't fuck me while all the time you were fucking them. Also it shows them what can happen when they mess with another man's wife."

"They know it was you."

"Of course they do, but they can't prove a thing and the next time you visit them you can tell them that there is more waiting if I ever lay eyes on them again."

"I don't know you anymore. You're not the man I married."

"And you my dear are not the woman that I married. That woman was not a fucking whore. But you are a whore Bess and I've decided that since I'm married to a whore I might as well get some benefit out of it."

"What do you mean?"

"Come on, I'll show you" and I grabbed her hand and pulled her along behind me and led her to the bedroom. There, sitting naked on the side of the bed was my boss. "You know Stan, Bess. Stan has always had the hots for you so I told him you would take care of him."

"You're joking."

"Not one bit my little whore. I've told Stan he can do anything he wants with you for as long as he wants. You don't have to do it of course, but if you don't you need to be out of this house within five minutes of saying no. The only thing you will be taking with you is a copy of the report and the pictures that I got from the detective I had following you. Have fun you two" and I turned and went back downstairs.

It was six in the morning when Stan came downstairs. I told him I would see him at the office and then I went on up to the bedroom. Bess was still lying on the bed and she looked up at me, "I suppose it's your turn now?"

"No thanks, I don't fuck whores."

"That's not fair Fred, you have no idea what I've been going through."

"And just whose fault is that? I forgave you and tried to forget; I offered you love and understanding and a shoulder to cry on and what did you do? You cut me off from sex so you could give it to those three assholes. I don't believe you were drunk that night when they took you out of the party and I don't believe that you didn't know what was going on. All I know is that you are a whore and that from now on, as long as you live under my roof anyway, you will fuck whomever I tell you to. You will be taking care of Stan and any of my customers that I want to take special care of. I'll make sure that you get plenty of cock Bess. I'll see to it that you won't miss those three assholes."

And I did. For the next three weeks I don't think Bess got dressed as I ran a steady stream of men through the bedroom. One morning Bess asked, "How long is this going to go on?"

"Until you get tired of it and leave."

"Are you telling me that there is no chance of us fixing up things between us?"

"I don't see how Bess. Honesty up front might have helped. I probably could have lived with it if you had come home and told me something like after your gangbang you found out that you liked lots of cock. That I wasn't enough for you anymore and you needed some on the side to supplement what you got from me. But that's not what happened is it? You stopped being a wife to me and became a whore for them."

"Fred, I love you. I'm sorry for what happened and I'm sorry for what I did to you. I was confused, I was mixed up and I wasn't thinking straight. Give me a chance Fred and I'll prove it to you."

"You can try Bess. I don't think it will work, but as long as you are living in this house you can try."

That was six months ago and Bess is trying. She hasn't made any progress yet, but she tries and as long as she fucks the men I bring home she can keep on trying.

# End of the 2nd Story

# Anny's Initiation

Anny and I have been married for almost twenty years and we have both worked very hard at keeping ourselves in shape. Anny is a knockout and all my friends want to fuck her. How do I know this? Simple! One day over beers in my backyard my buddies and me got to talking about each other's wives. John told Harry that he would swap his wife for Harry's and then we all got into the discussion with the outcome being that we would all like to try out each other's wives. A couple of more beers and we came up with a plan. We decided to start with Anny. We figured if we could get her to go for it, she would go along with us to help get the other wives involved. To get her interested I began to bring home X-rated videos and watch them on the VCR. At first she thought it was disgusting, but eventually she got interested in what the men were doing to the women.

"Do they really do that?"

"Is that real or make believe?"

"God! How can she do that with three guys?"

Our sex life really started to pick up and we began to experiment with things she saw on the videos and wanted to try. We had never tried anal before, and she found that she loved it.

One night, as we were watching Peter North fuck some delicious looking blonde, and as Anny was sucking my cock, the doorbell rang and Anny opened the door to find John, Harry and Tim standing there. A bit flustered she let them in. At first Anny was embarrassed to be in a room with three other guys watching fuck films. The guys joked and teased us, but they sat down to watch with us and before long Anny was looking at tents in the guys' pants and loving every minute of it.

I had my hand under her skirt and was fingering her pussy when she surprised me by taking my cock out and going down on me in front of the guys.

I had thought it was going to take a while to work her up to things, but she was hot and ready. Harry moved behind her and started feeling up her pussy while the other two guys started stripping their clothes off. Finding no objection to his fingers Harry pulled her panties off her and stood up to take off his clothes. John moved to take his place and Anny moaned loudly as John slid his cock into her hot, wet box. He fucked her for several minutes as she sucked on me and the sight of him behind her helped bring me to a gusher.

I got up and the guys grabbed Anny and undressed her while I made a mad dash for the video camera. My friends got her clothes off of her and laid her down on the couch; they began to suck her tits and finger her pussy and ass.

God, it was beautiful; she whimpered and moaned as her body thrashed on the couch and soon John had her on her knees and was fucking her while she was sucking Harry's cock. For the next two hours we took turns with her and when my friends finally left Anny had been fucked in all three of her usable holes and she had loved it. As the guys were leaving she told them they could come back any time they wanted to - whether I was home or not.

As soon as they were gone I told Anny about the plan to get all the wives fucked by all the guys. She couldn't believe that I had deliberately set her up, but told me that she was glad that I had, and she would like to see the other wives get the same amount of pleasure. Actually, that's not what she said! What she said was:

"It will do those stuck up bitches good to have a bunch of cocks in them."

We started making plans to bring the other wives into the fold, but in the meantime Anny is getting fucked almost every day by Harry,

John, Tim, and of course, me. I'm so turned on by watching Anny that I'm starting to wonder if I want to bring in the other wives - it will cut down on Anny's action.

# End of the 3<sup>rd</sup> Story

# David and Diane

Things were a little frosty when I left the house that morning and they probably wouldn't be a whole lot better when I go home. This is a bad time of the year for me anyway. Everyone wanted to have a party; company Christmas parties, both mine and Diane's, half of our friends planning holiday parties and I am just not a party animal. Diane is pissed at me because I wouldn't go to her company party with her. She knows I hate to go to those kinds of parties; I didn't even go to my own company Christmas party. Besides, I had a legitimate reason not to go. The project I was working on was due in three days which means I not only had to work tonight, but also would probably have to work the tomorrow night too. Then there was the fact that her company decided to have the party on a Tuesday night. Hell, the next day was a workday for everyone so how much fun is anyone going to have anyway? And if being held on a Tuesday wasn't bad enough the party was being held at her boss's house and a creepier guy I have never met. The first time I laid eyes on the man I took an instant dislike to him. There is definitely something wrong with him - I could just feel it. When I finish up here I don't guess it will really kill me to run over and drop in on the party. Who knows, a couple of drinks in Diane to loosen her up and I might even get lucky when we get home.

*** 

I hadn't really expected to have a good time without David being here with me, but so far I was having fun. It sure didn't hurt that I was one of only two unescorted females at the party. There were seven single guys constantly keeping me out on the dance floor and keeping my glass full. I was beginning to think that I might even have more fun than I would have had if David had come. I was a little apprehensive about dancing with some of the guys since they seemed to have a bad case of roaming hands and some of their comments made me think that they thought that I was fair game since I came alone, but I was a big girl and I knew I could handle it.

When they heard that I was going to the party alone some of the girls at work had advised me against coming and when I had pressed for a reason they had just given vague answers like "You just shouldn't, that's all." And I wondered why more of them hadn't come to the party. After about two hours I began to get a bit of a buzz on and I decided that I needed to cut down on the booze and so I switched to plain ginger ale, but somehow my glass always seemed to have alcohol in it when I came back from the dance floor. All the whirling around out there was keeping me thirsty and I drank pretty much drank whatever was put in front of me.

Looking back on it later I probably should have paid more attention on what was going on around me, like when all the couples began leaving. What I did notice was that all of my dance partners were getting me under the mistletoe. At first I tried to break away when the kisses were more than just pecks on the lips, but as I had more drinks I began to loosen up a bit and I became more receptive to the tongues that were being slipped into my mouth and I even responded - what the hell, it was a party and a little harmless flirting never hurt anybody.

The first that I knew that I was in trouble was when Mark danced me over near the couch where five other guys were standing around talking and then pushed me so that I fell back on the couch. It caught me completely off guard and before I could do anything a mouth closed on mine and hands grabbed my arms and legs and I was helpless. A tongue snaked into my mouth and I felt my panties being pulled off and then my legs being pulled apart. I screamed but the mouth covering mine kept the sound from coming out. I tried kicking my legs and twisting my body to break loose from those holding me but they were too strong.

And then I felt it pushing at my pussy and I knew that someone was going to put his cock in me.

I tried one more time to try and break free and then I felt the cock push by the outer lips of my pussy. I arched my back to try and get away from it, but five pairs of hands held me firmly down. The top of my dress was pushed down and hands undid the snaps on my bra. I felt tongues on my nipples, the cock in me was driving hard and the tongue in my mouth was working on me. I tried to fight it, but my body was liking the attention; I felt hot, a fiery heat was in my loins and my hips started pushing up at the invading cock. I started to respond to the tongue in my mouth and at the same time I heard a voice say:

"I'm there, I'm there" and I felt a flood of warmth in me.

I felt the cock pull out and only seconds later another one was shoved into me. Mouths and hands played with my tits, the cock stroking into me and the tongue probing my mouth were all turning my body into an inferno. I didn't know what was happening to me, but whatever it was my body wanted it. My hips were pushing up, trying to get more of the cock in me and the hands holding my legs let go and I lifted them and locked them behind whoever it was who was fucking me. A voice said "She's into it now" and my arms were turned loose and I reached up and dug my nails into the ass of the man between my legs and I pulled him to me. The mouth kissing me pulled away and a cock pushed at my lips and I opened my mouth and accepted it.

*** 

I was sure that Diane would be happy to see me and that the argument we'd had this morning would be forgiven. I found the address and then found a place to park. I walked up to the front door and rang the bell and when no one answered I rang it again. When no one came after a minute or so I decided that the doorbell didn't work and I knocked. I tried the door handle and found that the door was locked. I took the paper with the address on it out of my pocket and checked it against the number on the house; I was in the right place and besides I had seen Diane's car parked out front. I walked around the side of the house and onto the patio and I was just about to try the patio door when through the window I saw Diane.

She was on a couch and she had her legs wrapped around some guy who was fucking her. She had a cock in her mouth and was sucking it while four other guys stood and watched while jacking themselves off. My God, that's my wife in there - how could she do something like that to me? Don't our marriage vows mean anything to her? I reached for the handle of the door and even as my hand closed around it I hesitated. What I was watching my wife do was the most exciting and erotic thing that I had ever seen. Seeing my wife being a slut was turning me on in a way I would never have believed possible.

I saw the man who was in her mouth pull his cock away from her and I saw a rope of cum hanging from its head and I knew that my wife had just taken another man's load down her throat. I had my cock out and I was stroking it as another man stepped forward and pushed his cock in her mouth. I watched for several minutes and then my cock throbbed as cum gushed out of it as I watched the man fucking her move aside and let another man in. I saw Diane's hands come up and pull the man to her. I watched as two more men took her mouth and three more emptied themselves into her pussy. I had cum twice on the patio stones and I couldn't bring myself to watch anymore of what she was doing. I went home to wait for my slut wife to come home.

*** 

I felt myself being pulled off the couch and my dress was removed. I was pushed down onto my hands and knees and a man moved up behind me and speared my pussy and as he pushed in I pushed back to me him. In my new position I saw some of the other things that had been going on in the room. I saw my boss's wife watching two men fuck her eighteen-year-old daughter and I thought, how depraved is that? I saw my boss talking to the teenaged daughter of Stu Hansen as Stu and his wife stood off to the side and watched. I saw my boss take the young girl by the hand and lead her toward the back of the house and I suddenly knew who the new vice-president of sales was going to be. A few seconds later Stu's wife followed my boss and her nineteen year old daughter down the hall and my boss's wife went to her knees in front of Stu.

Then a man moved in front of me and all I saw was the cock he was moving toward my mouth. Things became a blur as cocks were pushed into my pussy and mouth and as I had orgasm after orgasm. Then my mouth was free for several minutes and I saw Stu's wife and daughter come from the back of the house and I noticed cum stains on both of them. I saw the bosses wife and daughter lying on the floor next to each other as they did what I was doing - take on any cock that wanted a hole to root around in. Another hour went by and then the women were alone in the room and as I struggled to get to my feet. the boss's wife came up to me and told me that I was a very welcome addition to their 'extended family.'

Only then did I fully realize the full extent of what had happened to me. True, I had not started of my own free will, but after it did start I became an active participant who did not want it to end and I spent most of the rest of the evening being an absolute slut - and I had loved it! Now I was being told that I would be invited back to do it again, and often. I was surprised to find that not only did I want to do it again - I was looking forward to it. I found my panties, bra and dress. My nylons were in ruins so I peeled them off and put them in my purse and then I dressed. I was headed for the door when Dora came up and took my keys away from me.

"I would not be a good hostess if I allowed you to drive in your condition. I'll have the chauffeur run you home. Henry will see to it that you are taken care of."

Henry helped me into the back of the limo and then pulled away from the house only to turn into the drive that led back to the seven-car garage. Stopping the car Henry got out and climbed in the back with me.

"I watched you from the patio and I saw how much you liked all that cock, but not one of them could do you justice. This one will" and Henry took the largest cock that I had ever seen out of his trousers.

I was stunned by the size of it and I reached out to touch it. It throbbed in my hand and I felt a charge, like a mild electric shock run through my body and the only thing I could think was "Thank you David for not coming tonight."

Henry fucked me twice and both times my body was nothing but a shivering, massive, continuing orgasm and I felt a huge disappointment when he moved back to the front of the car and drove me home. When we pulled up in front of my house Henry's eyes met mine in the rear view mirror and he saw what was in them and he got in back with me.

***

I was sitting at the window and watching for Diane when the limousine pulled up out front. I saw the driver get out to open the door for her, but instead of Diane getting out of the car the driver got in. When after two minutes no one emerged I knew what was going on. Even though I couldn't see through the tinted windows I knew Diane's legs were kicking in the air and that her nails were dug into the man's ass as she pulled him deep into her unfaithful cunt. I had been sitting at the window for over two hours waiting for her to come home and now that she was here I was surprised that what was upsetting me most was that I could not see what was happening.

It was twenty-five minutes before Diane got out of the car and walked toward the house and I got up and went into the bedroom. I pulled the covers over me and pretended to be asleep. I would wait until Diane was in bed and then I would reach for her and listen to her try and explain away what my hand would find. But her head no sooner hit the pillow than she began the light snoring that told me she was asleep. I reached over and shook her but she didn't respond. I rolled her over onto her back and shook her again, but she was out of it. I turned on the bedside lamp and pulled the covers off of her and saw that she had on a nightgown. Diane always slept in the nude and I wondered why she wasn't tonight. I lifted the gown and saw that her pussy was a wide open gaping hole and it was leaking cum, a lot of cum. She must have decided to keep her cunt covered so I wouldn't see it and to also keep most of the cum from staining the sheets.

I looked at the wide-open chasm between Diane's legs and the sight fascinated me. I reached down and touched the puffy, reddened lips and Diane gave a little moan. I stared at the hole for a bit and then I knew that I had to know what she felt like. There was no resistance as my hard cock slid into the hot, wet swamp that used to be Diane's tight pussy. As I began to fuck her I felt no friction; it was almost like pushing my dick into a bowl of hot water and I couldn't believe how sexually exciting it felt. I fucked her three times as I tried to imagine how many men had fucked her and for how many times and as I drifted off to sleep I wondered if tonight was the first time that Diane had done this. In the morning I awoke to the smell of fresh coffee and when I rolled over I found that I was alone in the bed. Diane had gotten up first and had covered up the evidence. I wondered how I could confront her without telling her that I knew what she had done. Admitting that I had seen it happen at the party would only bring a response of:

"Why didn't you do something? You could see that I was being taken against my will."

The fact that from where I was standing she was a more than willing participant would mean nothing. No, I couldn't go there. I decided that she wouldn't tighten up by tonight - she would still be pretty loose when we went to bed - and we could have the confrontation then. After breakfast and some chit chat about how boring the party had been for her she asked me to drive her to get her car. The butler answered the door and let us in and then he went looking for 'Ms. Dora' to see what she had done with the keys. Dora herself brought the keys and told me she was sorry that I hadn't been able to make it to the party:

"But we took very good care of Diane, didn't we dear?" and I saw Diane blush.

I walked her to her car and told her I would see her back at the house. In my rear view mirror I saw Diane get out of her car and begin to walk up the driveway. A quick glance showed me that there was a man washing a car there. It was the same man who had climbed into the back of the limousine with Diane last night.

\*\*\*

I was getting in the car when I saw Henry washing a car in front of the garage. I felt a tingle in my pussy as I remembered how full he had made it feel last night. I knew that last night had been a mistake and that I should never let myself be caught in a position like that again, but I only hesitated a moment before getting out of the car and heading up the drive. He shut off the hose when I walked up to him and dropped the rag he was using into a bucket on the ground. I thanked him for getting me home safe last night and then I asked him for a glass of water. He took my hand and led me into the garage and then upstairs to his quarters. He took a glass out of the cupboard and handed it to me and I walked over to the sink and began to fill the glass. Henry moved up behind me and I felt his hands go around my waist and his bulge press against my ass. I felt his hot breath on my neck and the he said:

"We both know what you really came up here for."

He started lifting my skirt and I closed my eyes, spread my legs and bent forward over the sink. As Henry's cock pushed aside the thin panties and split my pussy lips I moaned:

"Yesss, oh God yes."

I unbuttoned my blouse, pushed down my bra and began to roll my nipples between my fingers as Henry pushed his huge cock into me. I had never felt so full and as Henry pounded into me I had an orgasm. I heard a strange voice say:

"Hot little bitch, isn't she?"

I turned my head to see a man standing in the doorway. Henry said, "That's Tom. He's the gardener and my roommate. You're going to like him, his cock is as big as mine."

As I watched Tom undress and as Henry fucked me I wondered what had happened to me. Fifteen years as a faithful wife and then, almost instantly, a cock crazy slut. As Tom's cock leaped free of his pants I gave a low moan and motioned him over to me. I tried to take his cock in my mouth, but I could just barely manage to get my lips around its head. I felt the hot flood of Henry's cum and then he and Tom picked me up and carried me over to the bed. My legs were up on Tom's shoulders and he was fucking me hard when I heard:

"My, my, my. So nice to see that you like it here." Out of the corner of my eye I saw Dora standing there taking pictures with a digital camera. "I'm sure that we will be seeing a lot more of you. You just keep taking care of Henry and Tom while I go and get Roger. We do want to make your day a memorable one" and she turned and went down the steps.

Henry grinned, "Roger is the butler and you're going to love him. His cock is bigger than Tom's or mine. And then there is Rudy, the Chef. The Mistress hires the help based on cock size. When she gets back with Roger you will probably have to scoot over and make some room for her."

I moaned at the thought and my cunt squeezed Tom's cock as I had another orgasm.

\*\*\*

I looked at my watch for the fiftieth time. It has been over six hours. Where the hell is Diane?

# End of the 4<sup>th</sup> Story

# Wimpy White Ass

It started out innocently enough. Carolyn and I had been married for just a little over seven years and while we were happy together the bloom had left the rose as far as sex was concerned. I didn't understand it. Carolyn was beautiful, sexy and a fun person to be around, but the passion, the pure lust we had experienced in the beginning was gone.

At first it was two or three times a day every day and then over the years it had gradually slowed down until it was once a week or even once every two weeks. We went from chasing each other around the house and ripping each other's clothes off to "You want to?" "Sure, why not." It wasn't just one sided either. Whatever it was that was affecting me affected Carolyn also; she seemed just as disinterested as I did. It wasn't mental or physical because I constantly got erections from seeing other sexy women and I'm pretty sure from the expressions on Carolyn's face when she eyed other guys that she was experiencing the female counterpart of me getting an erection.

I was whining about it one night while I was having a beer after work with my partner.

"Hell Jim, all that's going on is that you and Carolyn have gotten used to each other – you are taking each other for granted. All you need to do is stir the pot, throw some shit into the game."

"Like what?"

"Damned if I know Jim. I don't know that much about your personal life to even say. Do you and Carolyn have oral sex?"

"Yeah, we do, or at least we did."

"How about anal?"

"Yeah, we have done that."

"Got a kinky side?  Want to watch her with some stud or anything like that?"

"Good lord no."

"Ever want to try any of the weird stuff like maybe peeing on her or having her pee on you?"

"No, never even thought about anything like that and the thought of it now makes me shudder."

"Well you need to find something Jim because it won't get better on its own."

I knew Hal was right, but knowing he was right and knowing what to do about it were not the same thing.

***

I thought about the problem, I thought about it a lot and I couldn't seem to find a solution.  I couldn't come up with any ideas until the night of Carolyn's birthday.  Carolyn and I were supposed to meet in the bar at the Hilton and then have dinner and take in a show.  I got a last minute phone call at the office that hung me up and I was a half-hour late getting to the Hilton.  I walked into the bar and spotted Carolyn sitting at the bar and talking to some guy.  From his body language it was obvious, at least to me, that he was hitting on my wife.  It was equally obvious that she was not chasing him away, but then there was no reason why she should.  She got hit on a lot and I knew that she could handle herself.

Normally I would walk up and Carolyn would say, "Oh, here's my husband now" and then she would introduce us and he would fade away.  For some reason this time I just moved to a table in a dark corner and sat down and watched.  The man took the stool next to Carolyn, waved the bartender over and ordered them both a drink. It was about five minutes before he made his move – he put his hand on Carolyn's leg just above her knee. Carolyn angrily pushed it away, but in the millisecond between his touching and her reacting my cock sprang to attention.

I have no idea what lay behind it because I had seen men make passes at Carolyn lots of times and it never gave me a hard on. I'd seen her kissed under the mistletoe at Christmas parties and it never affected me, but this guy putting his hand on Carolyn's leg had pushed a button. As soon as Carolyn reacted to the man's touch I got up and went over to them.

"Hi sweetie. Sorry I'm late, but I got a phone call just as I was walking out the door."

"No problem, in fact you are just in time to stop me from making a scene. Let's go."

She got up and we headed for the dining room and when we were seated I asked her about her 'making a scene' comment. And she told me what had happened.

"I know, I saw it" and then I told her about my coming in and watching. "But I don't understand the 'scene' part. You've always had men taking shots at you."

"Yeah, but never as crude as that slime ball. "Come on honey, I've got a room here and a ten inch cock that just drives women wild" and then he put his hand on my leg and I almost tossed my drink in his face."

"Too bad he was such an asshole; I would have been interested in seeing what would have happened had his hand moved a little higher."

"What?"

I reached under the table and took her hand and carried it to the hard lump in my pants. "That's what happened when I saw him put his hand on your leg. I'm just wondering if it would have ripped its way out of my pants had he gone any higher."

"Oh my, you nasty boy you. I think we should skip dinner and the show and just hurry on home" and that is just what we did.

We didn't talk much on the way home because Carolyn was stretched out across the seat with her head in my lap and with her tongue doing interesting things to my cock. We raced into the house and up the stairs to the bedroom and then we had the most satisfying sex we'd had in a long time. We made love five times and when it was over and we had snuggled up to each other Carolyn said, "What do you think would have happened if he had gone farther?"

"No idea. My reaction to his hand on your knee surprised the hell out of me. I've no idea of what higher might have caused. Why?"

"Because I'm curious. I'm turned on by you being turned on. Had I known this earlier we could have had some very interesting evenings."

"How's that?"

"I've had hands a lot higher than that on me and in more intimate places. If I'd known the effect that it had on you I would have let you know and I probably could have maneuvered things so you could have seen it happen."

"Why am I just finding out about these things now?"

"Because I assumed that you would be like most other husbands and go roaring off and punch the guy in the mouth and that would have cut our party invitations way down."

She reached over and fondled my limp dick, "I know it has been a long night for you lover, but any chance you can get it up again?"

"Maybe later babe, but I think you have pretty much drained me up to this point."

"Pity. Do you think that you could have gone again if I had spread my legs and let his hand travel a bit?"

My cock twitched and Carolyn giggled and said, "I think we have found a way to spice up our lagging sex life."

We spent the next couple of nights experimenting. She told me about all the times she had been felt up at parties and by whom, and how far she had let them go before shutting them down, but none of that had any effect on me. We finally decided that there were two possibilities for what caused my erection on Carolyn's birthday: Either it was because he was a stranger – someone I didn't know – or it was because I saw it happen.

"So," Carolyn asked, "Do you want to find out which one it is?"

I caught the inflection on the word "you" so I said, "You mean do we want to know, don't you?"

"Oh no sweetie, this one is on you. You get to make the decision here. Yes, I am curious about what it is that has caused our sex life to catch fire again, but the choice is yours lover, yours and yours alone."

"Why? Why me alone?"

"Because my sweet, the only way we can find out the answer is to put me out there as a guinea pig. I'm going to have to let men feel me up, try to get me hot enough to follow them to a back seat or a motel room while you watch. I can handle that – I've had to since I was thirteen – but can you handle it? I'm not about to do something and then come home and have you call me a slut or a whore for something I did. I'm the one who will have hands on her ass, hands on her tits, hands trying to run up her legs under her skirt and who will almost surely have tongues shoved down her throat. If you can handle my doing it I will do it, but you have to be the one to say "Okay Carolyn, let's go find out."

"That might be Carolyn, but you still have to want to know and tell me that you would like to know before I make the decision, I'm not going to do it just to satisfy my curiosity."

"Fair enough. Yes I'm curious and I would like to know."

"Okay Carolyn, let's go find out."

* * *

Our first attempt at finding out what it was that caused my hard on took place without my knowing. On Wednesday Carolyn stopped after work with three of her girlfriends. They got hit on and after several drinks they danced with some guys and then Carolyn let herself be separated from the group. The guy took her to a dark booth in the back of the bar and he tried to hustle her between dances. When she got home she told me what had happened. They had swapped tongues and she had let him get a hand inside her blouse and play with her right breast before she shut him down and went back to join her friends.

"Well lover, does that put any life in the noodle?"

"Some. We will definitely get a trip to the bedroom out of it, but I'm nowhere near as charged up as I was the other night."

Friday we attended a party thrown by some friends of ours. According to Carolyn there were seven guys at the party who had tried to get into her pants at one time or another.

"Keep an eye on me lover. Before the night is over I'll let one of them get me outside on the patio, be where you can watch."

About three hours into the party she came up to me, "You need to get outside. I told Billy I'd meet him out there in about five minutes."

I went out the front door and around the house to the back yard and found a place behind the garage where I had a good view of the patio. Billy came out and a couple of minutes later Carolyn came out. They stood and talked for a couple of minutes and then Billy pulled Carolyn to him and kissed her. She returned the kiss and Billy lowered one hand to Carolyn's ass and the other started working on her tits. Carolyn just stood there and kissed him and let his hands run free. Then Billy's hand left her ass and went to his fly and he pulled out his erection, took Carolyn's hand and placed it on his cock. She held it for maybe twenty seconds while stroking it and then she broke free and went back into the house.

I went back around to the front door, went inside and looked for Carolyn. I found her coming out of the bathroom, "Get me out of here lover," she said, "I don't know if it did anything for you, but I'm hotter than a forest fire and I need to be fucked and soon."

We had good sex that night, but it still wasn't the intense sex that we'd had the first time.

The next night, Saturday, found us in the parking lot of a bar. "How are we going to do this?" Carolyn asked.

"You go in and I'll give you twenty minutes or so and then I'll come in and find a seat where I can watch and we will see what happens."

"How far should I let it go?"

"Whatever you are comfortable with."

"No baby, you have to set the limits."

"It's a place of business Carolyn. He isn't going to take you on a table."

She got a wicked grin on her face, "So it's okay to duck under that table and give him a blow job?"

"You know what I mean Carolyn. Besides, if I'm right and it is the hands of a stranger on you that is the turn on I'll have you out of there and on our back seat long before you get to the blow job stage."

"Oh I don't know about that lover. If I get hot enough quick enough I can get to the blow job stage in a hurry."

I gave her thirty minutes and then I followed her into the bar. At first I didn't see her, but as my eyes adjusted to the low lighting I spotted her and a guy sitting in a booth along the back wall. I got a seat at the bar where I could see the booth and then I sat there and sipped beer and watched while they sat there, drank and talked. Occasionally they got up to dance and I began to think that the evening was a bust and I began thinking of ways to end it.

They had just finished a dance and the man had walked Carolyn back to their booth and then he headed for the men's room. On an impulse I followed him. I was standing at the urinal taking a whiz while I watched him feed quarters into the condom machine on the wall. He obviously thought something was going to happen so I decided to go back to my seat at the bar and watch just a little bit longer.

I was back on my bar stool before he got back to the booth and I watched as he slid in next to her, said something and then put his arm around her and pulled her tight against him. He kissed her and she returned it. They necked for a couple of minutes and then it happened. His hand moved to her right breast and squeezed it and I was instantly hard as an iron bar. I knew that I had found what we had set out to discover – it was the hands of an unknown stranger on my wife that had caused the intense sex that we had enjoyed that first time and that was lighting me up this time.

All I had to do was get Carolyn out of there without causing a scene.

In the booth I saw the man start to run his hand up Carolyn's leg. He took his other hand off of her tit and used it to take her hand and carry it under the table and Carolyn broke the kiss and looked over at me. She saw me watching and she gave me her evil grin and I saw her arm begin to move and I knew that she was stroking the guy's cock.

I nodded my head toward the bathrooms and got up and headed down the hall to the men's john. A minute later Carolyn came down the hall toward me and said, "Well?"

For an answer I took her hand and placed it on my erection and then I pulled her out the back door. I took her on the back seat right there in the parking lot and then stopped twice on side streets on the way home. Once we got home we screwed all weekend long.

Carolyn and I sat down and had a long talk about where we should go from there or if we should go anywhere from there. What it was doing for me was great, but I was concerned about what it was doing for her, or more to the point, to her.

"Don't you worry about me lover. It isn't bothering me at all because I know what it is doing for us. As long as you are sure that you are okay with what I'm letting be done to me. I'm having a good time with this. I get the best of both worlds; I get to fool around with other guys and then have you try and fuck me to death. But sweetie, and this is a big but, I still need to know how far you want me to take it."

"What do you mean?"

"Saturday I had the guys cock in my hand and I was stroking it. His fingers were on their way up my leg and had almost reached my pussy. How far do I go? Who stops it, you or me? The timing was good Saturday, but what if something happens and you get delayed? Do I keep whacking the guy off until he cums? I can't stop and start like a tape in a VCR. I can't start and then say, "Okay, we have to stop because my husband isn't here yet. Oh, there he is now, let's start again." What if you are sitting there watching and someone you know comes in and sees you and joins you and you can't break loose? Do I keep going? Do I stop, go to the ladies room and then sneak out the back door and sit in the car and wait for you? You have to set the limits for me sweetie, you have to define things for me."

"I told you once before, just do what you are comfortable with."

"Can't you get it through your thick head that this is not about what I am comfortable with? It is all about what you are comfortable with. It is all about you facing me when it is over and not thinking that I'm a fucking whore. I'm doing this for you. Granted, I am having a hell of a good time with you when we get home, but still, what I'm doing is for you."

"I thought it was for us"

"Okay, in a way it is for us, but I don't need it. I enjoy myself when you make love to me the regular way – without you being stimulated by an outside source, but you make love to me a hell of a lot more when you have been stimulated. So make love to me three or four times a week and we won't have to play games. The only reason I'm doing this lover is that our sex life was in the toilet until that stranger put his hand on my knee. Give me a sex life and we can stay out of bars."

"It isn't that simple for me. I could give you the three or four times a week and while it would be enjoyable it wouldn't be the intense "fuck all weekend" sex that we just had. I don't want the make love, cuddle up and go to sleep sex we used to have. I want the anywhere, everywhere, can't keep hands off non-stop sex we just had. We didn't have it when you fooled around with the guy the night you stopped with the girls and we didn't have it following what you did with Billy. We had sex, but nothing like what we had after the two strangers."

"Fine sweetie, but that brings us back to my question. How far do I go; what are my limits? Understand me here lover, I am a natural born cock tease and I enjoyed leading Billy and the man from Saturday night on and then leaving them hanging. My rings are on open display so they know that I'm married and if they come after me anyway that makes them assholes and I don't mind leaving an asshole with a case of blue balls. If it will turn you on I will do anything you want except fuck them. Yes, I'll even climb in a back seat and suck the guy off if that is what you want me to do, but you have to tell me how far I can go."

"Okay, how about this? You just set the limit – no fucking! The rest is up to you. You aren't going to jack a guy off if you don't want to and you aren't going to suck a cock if you don't want to and you aren't going to let a guy's fingers get into your pussy if you don't want them there. If you are enjoying yourself – enjoy. If not, give me some signal and I'll get you out of there. By the same token, if I get uncomfortable with what I see I give you a signal and we will split. Good enough?"

"You would actually let me give another guy head?"

"Only if you wanted to. You don't ever have to, but if for some reason you want to, go for it."

Carolyn gave me a long look and then said, "Okay, if that's what you want. Next question, how often? Once a week, twice a week, every other week, once a month?"

We settled on every other week and never the same bar more than once every three months.

The next six months were wild and it is a wonder that I didn't wear the skin off my cock. I watched Carolyn get hit on by dozens of strangers and I saw them put their hands on every part of her body. I watched her get finger fucked, I watched her give hand jobs and three times I even saw her with a strange man's cock in her mouth.

The first time she did it I was both shocked and surprised, but it almost made my cock rip right through my pants. Carolyn told me that she had been stroking the guy under the table, "And he felt so huge that I just had to see it. Once I was under the table looking at it I knew that you were watching and wondering so I just had to give it a couple of sucks just to see what it would do to you."

What it did to me was drive me crazy and I was still fucking Carolyn like a crazy man two weeks later.

The second time I was going to meet her at a bar when I got off work and I was late getting there. She had been necking with the guy and stroking him under the table trying to keep him under control until I got there. I hadn't been there two minutes and the guy put his hand behind Carolyn's head and applied pressure. She had looked at me and when I didn't jump up and charge over she let him push her head under the table. She came out from under the table three minutes later and looked over at me and wiped her mouth with the back of her hand. The guy had cum in her mouth and she had swallowed it all. I got so charged up over that one that we went a month before going out looking again.

The third time she did it she had gotten up to go to the bathroom and I had followed her. "He wants me to go out to the parking lot with him. Should I do it?"

"Do you want to?"

"It doesn't matter what I want. The question is do you want me to?"

"Carolyn, if you didn't want to we wouldn't be having this conversation. So it is back to you. If you want to it is okay with me."

"Well sweetie, under the table he feels like he is a good ten or eleven inches long and I can't get my hand all the way around it. I would like to get a good look at it, but if I go out to his car with him I'll probably end up giving him a blow job."

"So go for it."

I couldn't get close enough to see all of it, but I watched Carolyn's head bob up and down for a good five minutes before her head came back up. They talked for several minutes and I saw Carolyn's arm begin to move and then her head went back down again and this time it was down for almost ten minutes before they went back into the bar. On the way home she told me that she was sorry that she had come up with the "no fucking" limit. "God he was big. I would have loved to see whether or not I could have taken all of him."

She rolled down her window and tossed out something.

"What was that?"

"His phone number. If I'd have kept it I don't know that I wouldn't have eventually called him."

Again, I couldn't keep my hands off of her for weeks. We were making love more that we had on our honeymoon and that is saying a lot.

The sex we were having was fabulous. Not a normal life style, but it worked for us. At least it did until the day I came home from a business trip a day early. I hadn't called Carolyn to tell her my plans had changed. I don't know why I didn't because I normally did. I guess it had something to do with the fact that it was Sweetest Day and I wanted to surprise her and take her out to dinner and a show.

There was a strange car in the driveway when I got home and the house was dark. The only light on was the one in the master bedroom. Why a strange car in the drive and a dark house? I let myself in the house and the first thing I noticed was the quiet. Then I saw the empty wine bottle and the two glasses on the living room coffee table. There was no one downstairs and so, walking softly as I could, I headed up the stairs to the second floor. As I reached the top of the stairs I heard a man's voice say, "That was outstanding."

"Thank you sir, and I do have to say that you were rather spectacular yourself."

"Why did you make me wait so long and when and how often can we do this again?"

"To answer your questions in reverse order, this is a one time shot and will never be repeated. As far as the waiting, you would have waited forever if I hadn't needed, for reasons that are none of your business, to find out if I could have sex with a man other than my husband."

"Oh come on Carolyn, you can't just shut me off like that. This big black cock of mine drove you wild. You can't tell me that you don't want it again."

"Of course I want it again and as many times as you can get it up between now and when we have to leave for work in the morning. But when we leave this house in the morning it is over. Now that I know what I needed to find out I should ask you to leave, but because of that huge black cock and what you just did to me with it I'm going to make a night of it. But it is still just a one shot deal. If that isn't good enough for you, you can get dressed and leave now."

"Oh no baby. I'll stay and take all that I can get and gamble that by the time morning comes you will be so hung up on my cock that you will be begging me to come back."

"Go ahead and gamble all you want, but as much as I loved the fucking you just gave me and as much as I'm looking forward to the fucking you are going to give me it is still only going to be a one time deal. I love my husband too much to have an affair behind his back."

"I don't understand that. What are we doing now if it isn't having an affair?"

"I told you Mike. For reasons that are none of your business I needed to find out if I could fuck a man other than my husband. Now, are you going to waste more time talking or are you going to put that absolutely huge and marvelous black pole in me again?"

"Well, it is starting to recover and a little help might just speed up the process."

"I suppose that I could do a little something although I only got about two inches of it in my mouth last time."

The man laughed, "By tomorrow morning baby, I'll have you deep throating this licorice stick."

I don't know why, given the things that we had been doing lately, but suddenly I felt betrayed. Carolyn had once said that she would do anything short of fucking another man and yet here she was doing just that. And I wondered what her statement about needing to know if she could fuck a man other than her husband had behind it. I stood there in the hallway outside of our bedroom listening to the sounds of Carolyn sucking a black man's cock and wondered what I should do.

The obvious thing for me to do was storm into the room and rain all over their parade. The problem with doing that was that even though Carolyn was a cheating whore I still loved her. I loved her deeply and a confrontation could have several possible outcomes, one of which could be the end of our marriage and I didn't want that; at least not just then. Maybe it would come to that any way, but I wasn't going to rush it.

Discounting confrontation left me with only a few other options. I could slink away, not let Carolyn know that I knew; I could stay and listen and see where that would take me; I could try and find some way to watch and see where that led, or I could just walk into the room and say, "Oh wow, cool. I'll just go over and sit on the chair and watch."

Watching was out. There wasn't any way that I could get into a position to see without the possibility of being seen. I was not going to leave my own house like a whipped cur with my tail between my legs and walking into the room and pretending that everything was cool wouldn't cut it either because it wasn't cool, not by a long shot. So I made the decision that in the end killed my marriage to Carolyn. I decided to stay and listen and see what else I could find out.

I very quietly opened the door to the spare bedroom, which was 'kitty corner' across the hall from the master bedroom. Leaving the door open a crack I got a chair and settled in to listen. At first I didn't hear much, but after a minute or so I heard the man say, "Oh yeah baby, you sure do know how to suck a cock."

I was angry! I was very angry that my 'so-called' loving wife was in our bedroom giving a blow job to an unknown black asshole. I know that to some the situation would be considered laughable since I had already seen my wife with another man's cock in her mouth, several times, but the situations were not the same. In the first instance she was teasing the man for my benefit and when the time came she got up and left the guy hanging and then we went and fucked our brains out. Here, she was doing it behind my back – she was cheating on me!

Across the hall I heard, "That's enough baby; I'm hard enough and I want to get into that tight white pussy."

"Go slow lover, take it easy, I'm not used to something that big."

"That's a shame baby. Fine pussy like you deserves a great cock."

"Oh God, slow lover, go slow, let me get used to it." Several moans and then, "You're big, oh God but you're big. Oh yes baby, like that, push it in, give me all of it."

More moans and then the 'slap, slap' of flesh smacking into flesh and sharp little cries of pleasure.

"Jesus but you are tight" and then he laughed, "But only for me. Hope your hubby doesn't come home too soon and want to fuck. He won't even be able to touch the sides."

There was a loud moan followed by a sharp cry that I knew only too well – Carolyn had just had an orgasm.

"Oh god, oh god, so full, I'm so full, fuck me honey, fuck me hard."

"What's the matter baby, hubby doesn't do a good job of filling you up?"

"Oh God, oh sweet Jesus, so good, fuck me, please keep on fucking me."

"I asked you a question baby and I want an answer. Does hubby do a good job of filling you up?"

"Just fuck me, please baby, just fuck me."

"Okay. If you don't want to answer I'll just stop and get dressed and get out of here."

"No, no, don't stop, please don't stop."

"Then answer me."

"No he doesn't fill me up."

"He can't fuck you as good as I can?"

"No, he can't fuck me like you do."

"Kind of wimpy huh?"

"Please lover, don't tease me, fuck me damn it, fuck me."

"I asked you if your husband is a wimp."

"Yes damn it, he's a wimp."

"He's got a wimpy little white cock?"

"Yes he's little. Please don't tease me lover, fuck me."

Lots more 'slap, 'slap" and a whole lot of moaning. There were several 'oh yes's and 'fuck me, fuck me's and at least four more orgasms before the man said, "Here it comes baby, here comes a load of chocolate sauce."

Then there was a lot of heavy breathing before the man said, "Your hubby ever get you off like that?" There was silence and then the man said again, "I asked you if your hubby ever got you off like that." More silence and then, "Okay, I'll leave."

"No, don't go, please don't go."

"Well?"

"No, he has never gotten me off like that."

"You know why don't you? Tell me why he hasn't."

"He has a little dick."

"A wimpy little white dick?"

"Yes, a little wimpy white dick."

"Get down there baby, get me hard again. I'm going to make you forget your husband's name before I leave."

I sat there and listened to two more sessions and the constants were the same. Carolyn's moans, cries of orgasm, and the man's constant goading of Carolyn into saying I was a little dicked wimp. I was boiling mad, not so much at Carolyn, but at the egotistical asshole nigger she was fucking. She never called me a wimp on her own; she merely repeated back to him what he told her to say.

"Your husband is a wimp with a little white dick isn't he?"

"Yes, he has a wimpy little white dick."

She was enjoying his large member and was saying what she needed to say to keep him from stopping. As far as I was concerned I did not find that at all threatening to my ego and I sure didn't see that as my wife having no respect for me. However that quickly changed.

It was their fourth fuck session since I'd been there and this time the asshole wasn't leading Carolyn in anything. He was pounding away at her and she was moaning, "Oh god, so good, so good, deep baby, fuck me deep, like that, oh yes, like that, oh sweet fucking Jesus yes."

"You like this big black cock?"

"I love your big black cock."

"You like the way I fuck you?"

"Oh God yes."

"You ever been fucked this good before?"

"No lover, never."

"You ever going to be happy with your husband after this?"

"No lover, no way his wimpy white ass will ever be able to satisfy me after this."

And that was that. The end of my marriage in five seconds. Five seconds was all the time it took Carolyn to say those seventeen words that drove a stake through my heart. I got up from my chair and headed on down the stairs to the living room and got my cell phone out of my briefcase. I hit the speed dial for the home phone and when it rang I heard Carolyn cry out, "Oh shit, why now? Hold on lover, it is my husband's nightly check in call."

"Let it ring."

"I can't. He always calls when he goes out of town. If I don't answer it he might start wondering why." Another second or two and then "Hello?"

"Just calling to let you and your big dicked friend know that you can go ahead and fuck together for the rest of your lives. I'm taking my "wimpy white ass" out of the picture."

"Oh God, where are you?"

"Right now I'm in the living room, but don't worry, I'm not going to get my shotgun and come up, I'm just going to get the fuck out."

"No honey, don't leave, please don't leave. Stay there and I'll be right down."

"Don't bother Carolyn, I'm going to take my wimpy little white dick and leave."

"No baby, please wait for me. I can explain."

"Maybe you could, but I can't un-hear what you said any more than you can un-say it. Goodbye Carolyn."

I heard her running down the upstairs hallway hollering, "Wait baby, wait" as the front door closed behind me. Then I went into the garage and got a shovel and started taking the windows out of the nigger's car and waited for him to come out and tell the wimpy white guy that he was unhappy about it.

# End of the 5<sup>th</sup> Story

# Christine's Cuckold

I am a reasonably successful lawyer with a firm that I won't name. Christine was my wife of almost ten years. I met her my first day at the firm where she also worked. She was a legal secretary and I was smitten when I took her some documents that needed to be typed and gotten ready for signature. After my first month with the firm I asked her to have dinner with me and she accepted. We got along well together, started dating each other exclusively and I eventually proposed, she accepted and we were married.

Chris kept her job until she became pregnant and then she resigned to become a full time mother. Our sex life was great until the baby came and then somehow it faded to the point where we only made love twice a week. That seemed to be sufficient for Chris and while I would have liked it a little more often, it was no big thing to me.

Like every lawyer everywhere my goal was to reach a partnership. I worked long hours in an effort to reach my goal and so for the next several years I devoted most of my time to my career, but I wasn't making much progress. My billable hours were high, my work way above average, but I had an aversion to kissing ass. I wanted to make it on my own ability. Other associates worked hard at making partner and most of them brown nosed something terrible. They kissed ass and sucked up to the senior members of the firm every chance they got, but I didn't. Maybe it was naïve of me, but I still thought I could beat out the brown nosers and ass kissers on ability and good hard work.

I didn't know for sure, but I thought that Frank, the managing partner, had taken an interest in me. He was always around, watching what I was doing and keeping track of me and I thought that was an indication that my hard work was paying off. This feeling was reinforced when I was assigned to work directly under Frank. My workload increased tremendously, but the cases I was assigned were high profile and quite a few of them took me out of town anywhere from two to five days.

Three years went by and the first of every year when the partners sat down and apportioned out shares I saw my piece of the pie getting bigger and bigger. I was sure that I was on the fast track and would make partner in the next year or two.

\*\*\*

I was returning home from a four-day trip to Dayton, Ohio. I had managed to get done in time to catch the twelve-ten flight instead of the seven-thirty flight I was scheduled to catch and as a result I got home seven hours earlier than expected. As I turned on to my street I noticed two cars in my drive and one of them was Frank's. What possible reason could Frank have for being at my house at that time of day? I had no idea, but my natural instinct was to expect that it was something that I wasn't supposed to know about.

I drove past the house, turned the corner at the end of the street and then parked. I got out of the car and walked back to the house. The house was a sprawling four-bedroom ranch on two thirds of an acre and I had plenty of trees and bushes for cover as I approached it. I went straight to the windows to the master bedroom. The room had two windows, one on the east side of the house and one on the north side. It was summer and daylight savings time so I would have light behind me if I went to the east window, but the north side would be darker and so that is the window I headed for. Because of the trees, bushes and the fact that the closest neighbor on the north side was over four hundred yards away we almost never closed the blinds on the north side of the house. That would allow me to see into the living room, family room and kitchen if I was wrong and there was some simple and innocent reason for the two cars in the drive.

One look in the window told me why twice a week sex with me was sufficient for Christine. Sitting on the bed and leaning back against the headboard was Maxwell Bynum. On her hands and knees and wearing only a pair of black high heels was my wife and behind her was Frank. Frank was boning my wife from behind while her head bobbed up and down on Bynum's cock. Several things happened in the instant I saw my wife servicing the two partners from my law firm: My marriage ended, my love for Christine died and I made partner although I was the only one who knew it at the time.

The fact that my love for Christine died relieved me of the need to go into the house and kick some ass although I probably wouldn't have done it anyway since it would have killed off my certain partnership. As I watched Frank fuck my wife and my wife suck off Maxwell I suddenly came to realize why Frank had me assigned to him, why he was always around and keeping track of me and why I got all of the out of town business trips. It was so he would know where I was at all times so he would know when it was safe to fuck Christine. That, to me anyway, meant that this had been going on for at least three years. I expected that as long as I didn't do anything to let them know I knew it would continue to happen. And I wanted it to continue, oh yes indeed, continue it must.

I stood there for a little over two hours and watched as the two men worked over Christine and the more I watched the more pissed off I became. She did things for them that she never had done for me. They took her ass, which is something she had always refused me. She swallowed their cum where she had always spit mine out into a wash rag, and she screamed and had orgasm after orgasms which she never had with me. Maybe it was because of sensory overload because of two men working on her at once instead of just me; I don't know, but it still pissed me off.

I saw the two men take turns on her ass, I saw Chris suck Frank's cock when it came straight from her ass and then the frosting on the cake so to speak, I watched Frank fuck her pussy while Maxwell plowed her ass.

I left the window, got in my car and went and found me a bar.

***

I went home at what was the expected time and found Chris sitting on the couch watching the History channel on TV as seven year old Bradley sat on the floor in front of her doing his homework. Christine jumped up, ran to me, threw her arms around my neck and kissed me.

"I'm so glad you are back honey, I've missed you."

I'll just bet you have I thought as I gave her a hug. As much as I wanted to push her away from me the time wasn't right. I had things to do that required she not be suspicious and even if that meant I cheerfully had to take sloppy seconds following Frank and Maxwell, so be it. And sloppy seconds I would get because Christine made it almost a point of honor to have sex with me when I came home from one of my trips.

We had sex twice that night, both times in the missionary position and there was no offer of oral sex, which I rarely got and not even a hint of anal sex which I never got. If I hadn't seen Chris with the two men that afternoon I wouldn't have known I was getting leftovers because she felt the same she always felt. It dawned on me that it was probably because I was always getting leftovers and that made me wonder if maybe the Frank/Christine thing went back even farther than when he took me under his wing. It was obvious that Christine had been putting an awful lot over on me so it was no great leap to wonder about Bradley's paternity and I put a DNA check down on my list of things to do. I fell asleep that night making lists instead of counting sheep.

***

The next day was a busy one for me. I had to have a meeting with Frank and brief him on the results of the Dayton trip. It was easy for me to be cordial and smile in his presence and I suppose it was probably because he and Maxwell had made me a partner though they didn't yet know it. Then I had to rush from my meeting with Frank to make a court appearance and it wasn't until three that afternoon that I was able to meet with a private detective. I told him what I wanted, gave him a key to my house, Christine's schedule and a retainer.

The next two months passed by quickly and one day late in May I had my final meeting with the detective and then I went home, retired to my home office and reviewed what I had to work with. I had made five out of town trips during that two-month period and Christine had entertained on each of those trips. I had audio and visual of my loving wife with not only Frank and Maxwell, but with two other senior partners, two junior partners and three associates who, like me, were scrambling for a partnership.

I watched Christine take them on in ones, twos, and threes and I watched her pull an eight-man train. That tape was extremely enlightening. In it Christine was the wanton sexual animal that I wished she had been for me. She was lying on the bed in a lacy black bra and panty set that I had never seen before. The bra was cut a way and her nipples poked out and the panties were crotchless. They were stiff with excitement at what was to come. She also had on thigh high nylons and high heels.

The camera panned the room and I saw seven men – naked men – standing and looking at her. I didn't recognize any of them so I assumed that the affair was something that Frank had set up for some clients. The camera steadied as whoever was working it locked it down on a tri-pod and then Frank moved into the picture. He moved to the bed and said:

"Get yourself ready for me."

Christine looked at him, smiled and then started working a couple of fingers into her pussy. She let out a low moan and worked the fingers in and out several times and then she rolled over and got up on her knees. Frank moved in behind her, lined his cock up with her hole and then pushed.

"Oh God yes" my wife moaned as Frank started fucking her.

One of the naked men moved in front of her and she opened her mouth so he could shove his cock in it and she started sucking him. Frank rammed himself into her and after about three or four minutes he called out:

"Next man get ready, we need to wind her up and keep her going" and then I saw his ass cheeks clench and then he was out of the way to let the next man in. The man in her mouth grabbed the back of her head and moments later he pulled out of her mouth and I saw a thin rope of cum string from Christine's mouth to the head of his cock before it broke and fell to lie across her chin. He backed away and another man moved in and claimed her mouth.

All eight came in her at least once before they started to get creative. One guy lay down on his back and Christine lowered herself down on him and another guy moved to where she could get her mouth on his cock. While she was taking care of those two a third man moved up behind her and began fingering her asshole. Chris took her mouth off the man she was sucking and looked back over her shoulder and said:

"You want to fuck my ass? I love it in my ass" and she leaned forward to elevate her ass so he could take it. He moved up behind her and started working his cock into her ass and she moaned and went back to sucking the man in front of her.

I was sick at seeing what she was doing, knowing that she had never been that wanton with me. Not that I would have been willing to share her, but my God, what sexual energy and I never got to experience it and never would. She looked incredible riding one man's cock while sucking another while a third worked his cock in her ass.

It went on for three hours and through it all Christine begged them to fuck her harder, to fuck her faster, to push their cocks in deeper and to make her cum. I watched that tape half a dozen times and it never failed to make my cock hard and make me hate Christine even more for what she had denied me.

In every tape I saw she was a wanton whore – the complete opposite of what she was with me. I had surveillance reports of several meeting at various hotels and motels between Christine and several of my firm's most important clients, which was an unexpected bonus. In short, my wife was the firm's whore.

In addition to having the detective watch Christine I had taxed him to find out as much as he could about all of the men who had been fucking my wife. His report was very interesting reading and caused me to do some digging on my own to fill in some gaps.

Frank was married to a very wealthy and extremely jealous woman who had on several occasions been overheard saying she would cut Frank's balls off and stuff them in his mouth if she ever found out he was cheating on her.

Maxwell had a trophy wife that he doted on, but he wasn't stupid. He knew the odds on a young and beautiful wife remaining faithful to a man as old as he was and he had a prenuptial agreement that would give her nothing in a divorce. Maxwell's eyes must have been going bad because he missed some of the fine print. In the event of his being caught being unfaithful the agreement became null and void which meant that she could take him to the cleaners. A little further digging on the part of the detective found that Maxwell's wife had a boy toy that she saw on Tuesdays and Thursdays so it was almost a sure thing that she would go after Maxwell if she saw what I had on video.

Of the other two senior partners Benton Foley was bi-sexual and met every Wednesday with a body builder named Bruce and I wondered if his wife knew that? Stanton North was having an affair with the wife of the CEO of one of our largest clients.

The two junior partners were both single and played the field so I had no direct leverage there, but they would be useful in case I had to demonstrate an overall pattern should the mess ever end up in court.

The three associates, Holbrook, Neubert and Moore were all

married and my revenge against them would be separate from what I had in mind for the partners.

Lastly there was the whore that I was married to. The DNA tests showed that Bradley was not my son. Had he been my son I would have kept Chris around, but absent my parentage of the boy she was destined for the trash heap although I did intend to fight for the boy. It wasn't his fault that his mother was a pig.

After reviewing what I had I made my plans and then I went to bed and slept like a baby.

***

Monday I was due in court for a trial, but on Friday I was able to get the judge to grant me a continuance so I decided that Monday is when I would lower the boom. That afternoon I walked into Frank's office and told him that I needed a meeting on Monday morning with all the partners.

"What is this about Mike?"

"I have come into some information that could destroy the firm. I need a meeting with all the partners so I can tell them what is happening so they can decide how they would like to handle the crisis."

"I need to know more than that Mike. I can't just go to the partners and say that an associate wants to talk with them."

"You are going to have to Frank and they had all better be there. If that sounds like a threat to you then good, because that is just what it is. All the partners in conference room A at nine on Monday. See you then" and I walked out of his office. I drove home and when I got there Christine was surprised to see me.

"What's wrong Mike? You never get home this early."

"It was a fairly slow day Chris. I had some time to just sit in my office and think about some things. Personal things. And then I decided I needed some answers that I could only get from you. For instance, most men I talk to say they make love with their wives three and four times a week so I'm curious as to why we only have sex that many times in a month."

"I guess the answer is that I don't care to have sex more often and you never seemed to mind."

"How about swallowing my cum on the few times you give me head?"

"I hate the taste Mike. When I suck you off you enjoy it so much I don't want to ruin the moment by rushing to the bathroom to heave."

"What about anal sex?"

"That is just too disgusting to even talk about Mike, let alone do it."

"You have never had the urge to try?"

"Good God no! Why these questions Mike?"

"Just curious Christine. I'm working on a divorce case right now and the facts of the case just made me curious about my own life. What's for dinner?"

I expected that Frank would try and talk with Christine over the weekend to see if she could shed any light on the way I behaved in his office so I hovered around her all weekend. I made sure that I answered the phone every time it rang. Three times Saturday and four times Sunday the person on the other end of the line hung up as soon as they heard my voice. Once on Sunday, after the second hang up, Chris said:

"Who was it?"

"Must be your lover," I said, "Because he hangs up as soon as he hears my voice."

"Don't be silly Mike," she said, but I saw something happen in her eyes.

***

Monday at nine I entered conference room A and found that Frank had managed to get all the partners there. I could tell from their demeanor that that most of them were not pleased, but I suspected that they would be even less so by the time I got done with my presentation.

"First off let me thank you all for coming to this little get together on such short notice, but as most of you have a large stake in this firm I felt that you might be inclined to want to keep it."

"Come on Mike, get to it, we don't have all day," Frank said.

"Right Frank, you are all very busy men as I have come to find out. As all of you know, it is the goal of every lawyer joining a firm to make partner. We work hard, put in long hours and do whatever we have to do to reach that lofty goal. Two months ago my making partner was assured."

I saw several of them look at each other with a question on their faces since they knew of no such decision being made.

"It happened like this. I came home from the Dayton conference early and found Frank and Maxwell fucking my wife. I was angry, but as much as I wanted to go storming into the bedroom and kill all three of them a little voice was saying, "Hold on Mike. Christine is obviously a whore and not worth going to jail over and on the other hand there is your partnership. How can they turn you down? You have them by the balls." Then of course it occurred to me that I really didn't because it would be their word against mine. I needed proof.

"It was obvious to me that Frank was controlling my movements to give him access to my wife and that when I was on the trips he sent me on he was helping keep my wife from being lonely. So I hired a detective agency, gave them the keys to my house which they promptly wired for audio and video."

I paused for a moment and looked around the room, "Aaah, I see from the looks on your faces that the penny has dropped. Look around guys, see what you all have in common. Every one of you, with the exception of Ben, Marty and Scott have been fucking my wife and I have it all on tape and in living color."

"What are you going to do?" Maxwell asked.

"Good question. When this started my plan was to make sure that you and Frank saw to it that I made partner, but once I found out the scope of what Frank had done the idea of partner went away. There isn't any way I could have a working relationship with all of you now. I could have handled it with only Frank and Maxwell, but I couldn't even try with as many of you as there are. In fact, I have no choice but to leave the firm. But I decided that if I have to go I am not going to go away empty handed. I don't believe that there has ever been a buyout for an associate, but there is always a first time for everything right?"

"You are right. It has never been done and it won't be done now. Clean out your desk and be out of this building by ten," Maxwell said as he started to stand up.

"I'm not done yet Max. Sit your ass down or be ruined, your choice."

He gave me a steely look, but he sat down.

"Once I decided I had to leave and wanting it to be both vengeful and rewarding at the same time I set the detective agency on each one of you."

I opened my briefcase and took out several large manila envelopes and handed each man the one with his name on it.

"In the envelope are copies of the original private detective agency report and photos of you and Christine. In addition there is a copy of the detective's report on you and what you have been up to along with a detailed description on what I intend to do with that information if I leave here unhappy. None of the others know what is in your own personal report although I'm sure that you all know what is in the original one. Let me spell it out:

-One. All of your wives will get copies of what you have in front of you and most of you can start looking for a good divorce attorney.
-Two. One of you is having an affair with the wife of the CEO of one of the firm's largest and most influential clients. The client will receive a copy of the evidence and I'll just let you use your imagination as to what he might do.
-Three. The wives of the five clients that Frank had Christine fuck will receive a copy of the evidence.
-Four. All of this will be leaked to the press.
-Five. All of the photos that were taken will be posted on the Internet, copies will be sent to the Bar Association and to every other law firm in the state. I have also printed out our entire client list and every one of them will get a copy of what is in the envelopes in front of you.

"In short gentlemen, you will become the laughing stock of the legal profession in this state and I would expect that your client base will disappear, which brings me to what I want in order to keep any of the just listed from happening. These are non-negotiable and will be agreed to no later than noon today or I will proceed with my plan to ruin all of you and the firm.

"First, the three associates, Holbrook, Neubert and Moore will be terminated by the end of the day and they will not, repeat WILL NOT be given letters of reference.

"Secondly, the terms of the buyout I mentioned. One million dollars for each of the partners, both senior and junior, who thought it would be fun to fuck my wife behind my back. That comes to six million and it will be paid in such a manner that I will end up with the entire six million after taxes.

"The last thing of course is the positively glowing letter of reference that the firm will give me. Said letter to be positively reinforced whenever someone calls with questions."

I closed my briefcase and looked around the room meeting the eyes of the few who didn't turn their face away. "Noon gentlemen. Now if you will excuse me I need to go and start cleaning out my office."

I hadn't been at it ten minutes when Frank came into my office. "You know that you won't get away with this."

"If I don't it will be too bad for you personally and for the firm in general. I meant every word I said in our little meeting. You made the mess Frank. You don't like messes you should have never started fucking my wife."

"Started? I never stopped. Christine was my bitch before you started working here and she's never stopped being my bitch. You're a chump Mike. I fucked her the whole time you dated. I fucked her at nine on the morning of the day you got married and I fucked her on the first day you were back from your honeymoon."

"You are stupid Frank if you think you can goad me into hitting you so you can press charges and give yourself some bargaining power. I'm not going to bargain on anything Frank. I said my piece and it is non-negotiable."

"Not much of a man are you Mike? I tell you your wife is my bitch and that I've been fucking her whenever I want and you take it. What's the matter Mike? No stones?"

I stopped what I was doing and looked at him for several long seconds and then I buzzed my secretary.

"Mrs. Henry, would you please get Mr. Bynum on the phone for me?"

Fifteen seconds later the phone rang. "Maxwell? Frank is in my office and after talking with him he has convinced me to drop my demands. I'm just going to go ahead and ruin you and the firm and be done with it. Tell the others will you?" and I hung up on him.

"Satisfied Frank?"

Before he could answer me the phone rang.

"Hello?"

"Yes, he is still here."

I handed the phone to Frank, "It's for you."

I have no idea what Maxwell said to Frank, but whatever it was it caused the blood to drain from his face. I heard him say, "Yes sir" a couple of times and then he said, "I understand" and he held the phone out to me.

"Yes Maxwell?

"No problem, but noon is still my deadline." I hung up the phone and looked over at Frank, "You still here?"

I was carrying a box of my stuff out to my car and I happened to walk by Bill Neubert's office. His door was open and he was cleaning out his desk. I couldn't resist the impulse and I stuck my head in the door.

"Was Christine's pussy worth it?" and then I walked away

without waiting for an answer.

I was packing my last box when the phone rang and it was Maxwell asking me to meet with the senior partners in the conference room. It was a bargaining session and they were finally able to convince me that the firm didn't have and couldn't get six million. I settled for three point four million deposited in a Cayman Islands bank. No hands were shaken at the conclusion of the deal and I got up, left the building and went home.

***

I was sitting in the family room watching CNN when Christine came home from wherever she had been. She came into the room and saw me sitting on the couch.

"You're home early dear. Is everything all right?"

"Everything is just peachy Christine. My life just got a whole lot simpler."

"What does that mean?"

"It means that I've decided on making some major changes in my life. I quit the firm today."

"Why on Earth did you do that? What are you going to do? How are we going to pay the bills?"

"I'm going into business as a distributor of porn videos. I understand that there is big money to be made in that field."

"Seriously Mike, what are you going to do?"

"I am serious Chris. Here, let me show you the first one I am going to distribute" and I pushed the PLAY button on the remote for the VCR. Christine's face went pale when she saw herself on the screen.

"Funny thing Christine, but I've watched this tape at least ten times and not once have I seen you run to the bathroom to heave after swallowing the cum from all those cocks. Another thing I noticed is that even though anal sex is too disgusting for you to even talk about you still manage to do a lot of it."

She looked down at the floor and weakly said, "What are you going to do?"

"Throw your worthless ass out and divorce you." I looked at my watch, "In fact Chris, the company I hired to move your shit out of here should be here at any minute now. I would assume that the man who will serve you with the divorce papers is driving the car that just pulled into the drive. I will tell you up front that you won't be getting a dime out of the divorce so you had better start looking for a job. I doubt that you can get back on at the firm, not after the bomb I laid on them this morning. I suppose Frank could be your pimp and you could make some money standing on a corner on South Avenue."

Christine just sat there staring at me woodenly.

"What's the matter Chris? Got nothing to say? Don't you want to tell me that it is somehow all my fault? How about that old standby, "But honey, I can explain." Or maybe you could take a shot at, "It isn't what you think."

"Also, before you waste your time thinking you have a little leverage because of Bradley you should know I had DNA tests run and I know that Bradley is not mine."

Christine had been looking down at the floor, but her head jerked up when I said that and I saw the surprise on her face. "Oh, you didn't know that? Good, now you have something to do in your free time. You can try and figure out who the daddy is. Go pack Christine. I want you out of here tonight."

"But where can I go?"

"Call Frank. According to him you were his bitch before I met you and you stayed his bitch the entire time we have been married so maybe he will take care of you. If he doesn't, tough shit! Just be out of here by tonight." I got up and walked out of the room leaving her staring at the floor.

It didn't end there of course.

Christine still had lots of family living and I'd warned her if she fought me on the divorce they would all get copies of some of her better performances and I specifically mentioned her eight man gangbang. But she did fight tooth and nail over custody of Bradley and I had not helped my cause any by letting her know that Bradley wasn't mine. In the end the court, as they so often do, gave the child to the mother and since I wasn't the biological father I didn't even get visitation.

As part of the agreement reached when the firm settled with me I had to agree to never divulge the information I had gathered and that I would destroy all copies of it. But being a lawyer I decided to play the "It depends on what the meaning of is is" game. Copies to me meant a 'copy of the original,' but not the original itself so I put all the 'originals' in a safe deposit box and destroyed all the copies. I was fairly honorable, but I didn't think I could say the same for my ex employers. I would hang on to the originals just in case they reneged on the agreement.

I said I would never divulge the information that I had gathered, but I never promised not to use what I had found. I started the rumor that the reason that Neubert, Moore and Holbrook had been let go was that they were caught playing fast and loose with a client's funds that had been entrusted to their care. None of the three ever got on with another firm and Holbrook and Neubert finally left town. Moore went into private practice, but I hear that he is having trouble paying the rent on his office. One of the things I did when I left the conference room was to place a pre-arranged phone call to a messenger service and copies of all the material I had that pertained to the three was delivered to their wives and the three were financially ruined by their divorces.

Frank set Christine up in an apartment and Frank's wife received an anonymous phone call telling her that Frank was cheating on her and she hired a private detective and he got her enough so that she could rape Frank in a divorce. When the dust settled Frank left town forgetting to take Christine with him and also forgetting to tell her where he was going.

Christine wasn't alone long as Maxwell took up where Frank left off. Maxwell's wife got a phone call from her boy toy one afternoon. It seems he was in a bar having a few drinks with some friends when he overheard one guy talking to another guy about what a lucky stiff Maxwell was to have such a beautiful wife and a hot mistress on the side. Maxwell's wife hired a private detective and I heard that she did quite well for herself in the divorce that followed.

Foley's wife got an anonymous tip about her husband's body building boyfriend and he was the next one to visit divorce court. I got all warm and fuzzy inside knowing that I was single handedly seeing to it that divorce lawyers and private detectives were making a good living.

Stanton North got a pass. There was no way to go after him without his affair with the CEO's wife coming to light and I had promised that I wouldn't reveal that. I know, I know, a tip to his wife and her private detective would have uncovered it, but my tip would have been responsible.

Now if I could only come up with a way to do something to those two junior partners. I'm working on it and I'm sure that something will come to me sooner or later.

# End of the 6<sup>th</sup> Story

# Cathy, Gloria and Me

It started out as a joke and then things kind of got out of hand. Not that I'm complaining mind you, because as far as I'm concerned it all worked out.

I had gone through a rough stretch, losing my job and my fiancée within two weeks of each other. I was down on life and I was down on women. I'd had a great job, one that I actually enjoyed getting up in the morning and going to. Everything was great right up to the morning I showed up for work, found the door locked and a notice taped to the window that said the IRS had seized the place for non-payment of taxes. The owner of the company disappeared owing all of the employee's wages and it was three weeks before I could even get into the building to get my personal possessions. Even then I had to prove to the IRS that the stuff was mine and not the company's.

I took the second hit nine days later when Karen, my fiancée, told me during dinner at Mike's Chop House that she was going to postpone the wedding.

"I've decided that it just wouldn't be fair to you to marry you right now," was how she put it, "Maybe later, but not now."

Naturally I was a little upset what with the wedding being only two months away and I pressed for a reason and she had them. Four of them in fact.

"I love you Rob, I honestly do and I know that you love me, but I guess the truth of the matter is that I'm not ready to settle down. I keep meeting interesting guys and wanting to get to know them better. On nights you've worked late or been out of town, I've dated."

When I pressed for a more detailed explanation I got much,

much more than I wanted. Joe, a guy she worked with, kept trying to get her to go out with him. She finally did and she enjoyed herself and so she went out with him again. On the sixth date he managed to get her in bed.

"It was a disaster Rob. He wasn't anywhere as good as you and when it was over I never went out with him again.

But Joe was followed by Alan who was followed by Tom who was followed by Jim. She swore that none of them were any good in bed and that none of them made her feel like I did.

"The bottom line Rob is that I'm still curious and just yesterday this really cute guy asked me for a date and I said yes. We need to postpone the wedding until I get this curiousness out of my system."

I asked her the time frame during which she was climbing into all these beds and she told me that it had been in the last two months. While we were planning the wedding and the honeymoon she had been bed hopping. I thanked her for telling me and then said that postponing the wedding was not the way to go; we should just cancel the wedding altogether and then I got up from the table.

"Where are you going?"

"Away from you Karen. You are apparently a round heeled slut and I don't need one of those in my life - now or ever."

She was crying when I walked away from her and whether it was from the knowledge that I never wanted to see her again or that I stuck her with the check I would never know.

\*\*\*

I started looking for another job. I was having lunch with my step-sister Cathy one day and she told me that they had openings where she worked.

"I thought that they had a policy of not hiring relatives of current employees."

"They do, but no one knows that you are my step-brother. My married name is different than yours so if you put down "no" in the section that asks if you have relatives working there they will never know."

"That's all fine and dandy Cathy, but we can't hide the fact that we are close."

"We don't have to hide it. If you get the job on your first day I'll act surprised as hell and then let everyone know that you are an ex-lover that I had let get away, but that I had never gotten completely over. That should cover any affection that people might see. It will be fun. I have a reputation as a 'goody two-shoes' and it will set some of the women on their ear, especially the gossipy ones, when the married lady takes long lunches with her ex-lover."

"A goody two shoes? You?"

"Yeah, me. I won't stop with the crew after work for drinks because the first time I did every guy in the office was trying to get me to go out to the parking lot with them and play the 'back seat bounce.' I don't care for that kind of stuff so I never stopped again."

"But as my ex-lover you will stop if I stop, is that what you are saying?"

"Probably. We might even give the gossips some good stuff to work with."

"How's that?"

"Imagine if you and I were to go out to the parking lot and then came back in later."

"Oh Cathy, you are indeed evil."

***

I did apply and I did get the job and things did pretty much go the way Cathy had outlined. We had lunch two or three times a week and we did stop about twice a week with the gang after work. There were at least half a dozen good looking women in the group and I had already picked one out, but when I mentioned it to Cathy she would have none of it.

"You're mine honey, at least until I've stood this group on their ear. After that you can spread as much pollen as you like, but not until I've had my fun."

The first night we stopped with the group she made sure she sat next to me at the table and when I made no move to get her out on the dance floor she grabbed my hand and dragged me out there. After a couple of minutes she maneuvered so her back was too the table and she asked me if the group was watching. I looked over her shoulder and saw that most of them were.

"Kiss me," she said.

"What?"

"Kiss me. You are an ex-lover who is still hot for me."

I went to kiss her on the cheek and she said, "Don't you dare! You're hot for me; make it look right."

You have any idea how weird it is to have your step-sister's tongue down your throat? To have her rubbing her body up against yours? How about when that rubbing gives you a woodie and your step-sister giggles and says:

"Wow, that gives a whole new meaning to "big brother."

When the music stopped she wouldn't let me go back to the table. "You need to get rid of that blush little step-brother and stop being so flustered before we go back. I'm a married woman who is still hot for an ex-lover and you are supposed to be still hot for me, not embarrassed."

Cathy had me put some more money in the jukebox and we stayed out for three more songs before heading back to the table. I saw the ladies at the table eyeing the tent in my trousers and I was wishing like hell that one of them could take care of it.

\*\*\*

We repeated that scenario the next two times we stopped after work and Cathy always managed to make it look like she was chasing me. Once at work, in front of three girls, she pulled me into a supply closet and then she kissed me to smear lipstick on me for the girls to see when we came out.

Cathy was having a ball, but I was suffering big time. She might have been my big step-sister, but she was still a good looking sexy woman. Being my step-sister didn't make her tits any less real when she rubbed them against me. Being related to me didn't make the pussy she kept rubbing against my leg or erection a fake one. Oh yes, she was giving the gossips a field day, but she was sending me home with a severe case of blue balls.

It all came to a head one Friday night when we stopped after work for drinks with the crew. We were on the dance floor and Cathy was up tight against me rubbing her tits against my chest and her crotch against my leg (and erection) and she whispered in my ear:

"Tonight's the night little step-brother. When we finish this dance we will make the trip to the parking lot. By this time tomorrow my 'goody two-shoes' reputation will be toast."

"I still don't understand why you are doing this. Why do you want your co-workers thinking you are a married slut?"

"Just being perverse little step-brother. They labeled me without knowing anything about me so I feel the need to stick it to them."

The music stopped and she led me back to the table where she said:

"You guys watch my purse, okay?" and then she led me out the door and into the parking lot.

"Now what?"

"We get in the back seat of your car and wait the proper amount of time and then go back inside."

We got in the back of my car and the door had just barely closed when Cathy said, "Oh shit!"

"What?"

"Harriet must not have believed her eyes. She followed us out and she's hiding behind a car watching us. Kiss me."

"What?"

"Kiss me damn it" and she grabbed my head and shoved her tongue down my throat. I just kind of sat there and Cathy said, "Come on Rob, help me out here, make it look good" and she kissed me again. "Come on Rob, make it look real" and so I kissed her back.

While we swapped tongues Cathy kept looking over my shoulder at where Harriet was hiding. Cathy broke the kiss long enough to mutter, "Stupid fucking bitch! Why doesn't she go back inside" and she went back to frenching me. A minute later she grabbed my left hand and put it on her breasts.

"Come on Robbie, we're hot for each other remember? Give her a good show."

So there I was on the back seat of my car pawing my step-sister's tit and she's frenching the hell out of me and suddenly Cathy decides that it isn't enough. She decides that Harriet needs to see us fucking. She broke the kiss, pulled her skirt to her waist and then lay down on the seat. She put her right leg over the front seat back and had her left up in the air and she said:

"Get down here Rob and pretend you're doing me."

I'm looking down at her and my eyes are locked onto her pussy. She had a little itty bitty thong on and her pussy hairs are curling out beyond the edges of the material. Cathy reached up, grabbed my shirt and pulled me down.

"Come on Rob, move your butt. Make it look like you're doing me."

She had pulled me down so that my erection was right against her mound. She kept after me to move my butt so I did and my hard cock was rubbing against her cunt. I don't know if it was doing anything to her, but I was about to lose it in my pants.

"Just one more minute Robbie, just one more minute."

Over my shoulder she saw Harriet at the window actually looking into the car and she wrapped her legs around me and started pushing her panty covered pussy up at my pants covered cock and her hands pulled my face down and she shoved her tongue in my mouth again.

There is a point where a man can be so sexually charged up that he stops thinking, or stops thinking clearly anyway. I was at that point.

Three weeks of play acting with Cathy and constantly going home with blue balls; the nights dancing, the frenching, Cathy's putting my hands on her tits and the fake sex on the back seat with my hard cock rubbing Cathy's pussy finally got me to the point where I lost it. It didn't matter to me anymore that she was my step-sister. She was a pussy already spread out on my back seat and all that was between my cock and what it wanted was a zipper and an easily pushed aside thong.

I pulled my zipper down and worked my cock out of my pants. I hooked a finger under the thong and pulled it aside and suddenly Cathy pulled her tongue out of my mouth and looked at me wide eyed.

"What are you doing? Stop that Rob, stop that right now."

My cock was poking at her pussy, trying to find a way in, and Cathy was struggling to get out from under me.

"Stop it Rob, stop it! Harriet is gone."

Then she slapped my face and hissed, "Get off me damn it." The blow caused me to shake my head which cleared it some and I got up from Cathy and sat on the seat with my hard cock sticking up out of my fly. Cathy sat up and screamed at me:

"Just what the fuck were you going to do? What kind of a pervert are you anyway? I'm your step-sister for God's sake. Just what kind of an asshole would try and take advantage of his step-sister."

I was sitting there, hard cock still standing straight up, as she verbally abused me and called me every rotten name she could think of and then I totally lost it.

"Me? I'm a fucking pervert? Just whose idea was it to play these stupid fucking games?"

I pointed at my hard cock, "You think I just willed that to get hard? You're the one rubbing your tits all over me, putting my hands on them and telling me to make it look good. You're the one who has been rubbing your pussy against my cock for three fucking weeks now. You are the one who was just humping your pussy up at my cock a minute ago so don't be calling me names."

"Listen you fucking assh..." and she didn't finish what she was going to say because I reached and grabbed a handful of her hair and pulled her head down. She opened her mouth to protest and I shoved my cock into the open hole and held her head in a death grip. I hunched up fucking her face a half dozen strokes and shot my wad. She had to gulp and swallow because I wouldn't let go of her head. As my cock started to go soft I woke up to the fact that I had just fucked up big time.

I dropped my hands and my cock fell out of Cathy's mouth. She jerked her head up and looked at me with hatred and disgust flaming from her eyes.

"You bastard! You dirty fucking bastard!" she snarled as she scrambled to get out of the car. I watched her walk into the bar and less than two minutes later she came out with her purse, got in her car and drove off. I sat in my back seat and stared after her until her taillights disappeared.

***

I don't know why I lost it and did what I did. All I knew is that it was wrong and that I had fucked up. Would Cathy go home and tell her husband Stan and would he come looking for me with a gun? Worse, would she tell our folks? She couldn't do anything at work except scowl at me or ignore me. She couldn't cost me my job without putting her own job at risk. After all, she was the one who spread the ex-lover story even though I was her step-brother. I didn't think that the powers that be in the company would take kindly to her trying to pull the wool over their eyes. No, all I had to sweat was mom, dad and Stan. And of course Cathy. She might even come after me with a gun.

It being the beginning of the weekend I decided that my best bet was to get out of Dodge. I drove home, packed a bag and headed for the beach. I checked into a motel and then spent Saturday and Sunday lying on the sand, soaking up sun and trying hard not to worry about what might be waiting for me when I home.

*** 

It was late Sunday when I got home and no one was sitting on my doorstep waiting for me and I took that as a good sign. No flashing light on the telephone answering machine either - another good sign. What wasn't good was trying to sleep that night knowing that I would be going into work in the morning and seeing Cathy. In the end that turned out to be a non-event. She ignored me.

For the next two weeks it was as if I did not exist as far as Cathy was concerned. If we were in the lunchroom at the same time she sat as far across the room as she could get and usually with her back to me. Wednesday of the second week I was in the lunchroom looking at Cathy's back when Darla sat down across from me. She saw where I was looking and she said:

"Trouble in paradise? A cooling of the relationship?"

Even though Cathy and I were not talking I still had to play the role. "She wants it both ways; she wants to be married to Stan, but still play with me. She got pissed when I told her I wasn't going to buy into that."

"Is the relationship going to heal?"

"It never should have started in the first place. When I came to work on my first day and saw her I should have just turned around and gone back to job hunting."

"Well, if she's history it might interest you to know that there are a couple of girls here who are interested in you. You should stop with the gang after work more often."

"It would be awkward with Cathy there."

"Shouldn't be a problem. She never stopped before you came to work here. If you've split I doubt that she will stop."

"Is this your way of saying that you are interested?"

"No, I'm spoken for, but because I'm neutral I can try and be a matchmaker. So, you going to stop tonight?"

"Don't know. I'll think on it."

\*\*\*

I did stop that night and I did have a good time dancing with the women there. I stopped again on Friday night and had such a good time that I asked Gloria to have dinner with me on Saturday and she said yes. Saturday's date led to a Tuesday date which in turn led me to spending most of my time dancing with Gloria when we stopped at the bar after work.

That Friday I was in the lunchroom at the same time Cathy was, but his time she didn't sit with her back to me and she watched me the entire time I sat there. In fact, she never took her eyes off of me. Ten minutes after lunch my phone rang. The read-out on the panel said the call was internal from extension 127. 127 was Cathy's extension. I stared at the phone and debated on pretending I wasn't at my desk and just let it keep ringing, but then I decided that I had to talk to her sooner or later and I might as well get it over with.

"Yes?"

"Why are you doing this to me?"

"Why am I doing what to you?"

"Making me into a laughing stock."

"And just how am I doing that?"

"By going out with that bitch Gloria."

"Just how in the hell is that making you a laughing stock?"

"You are supposed to be my lover. Going out with her has everyone snickering at me behind my back."

"Have you forgotten that you are married Cathy? And that I am your step-brother? You got what you wanted. No one thinks of you as Miss Purity any more. Besides, our office romance had to end sometime. Everyone in the office has seen how cool you have been toward me lately and they all think that you came to your senses and decided not to risk your marriage over me."

"You know full well why I have been cool toward you."

"Yes I do and I am sorry. I don't know what made me do what I did and I am ashamed of myself. I truly regret it and I'll be apologizing for my behavior for years to come, but at the same time I'm not going to forget who led me to the edge and helped push me over it. It had to end and it has."

"But it didn't end the way it was supposed to. I was supposed to drop you in a way that let everyone know it was me letting you go, but now everyone is laughing at me because they think that Gloria took you away from me."

"Cathy, get a grip on yourself" and I hung up on her. The phone rang several more times and the panel showed that the calls were from extension 127 so I didn't pick up.

\*\*\*

I was surprised to see Cathy at the bar when I stopped that night. As usual the crew had put three tables together to make one long table and Gloria was sitting at one end and Cathy was sitting at the other. I immediately knew I was in trouble. If I sat near Cathy I could kiss my burgeoning relationship with Gloria goodbye and if I sat with Gloria only God knew what Cathy might do. The third choice was to sit in the center well away from both of them, but that would just tell everybody I was a coward.

As I approached the table it dawned on me just how stupid I was being. Why was I even thinking about choices? On the one hand there was a woman I wanted to get to know better and on the other was my step-sister who was playing games. I sat down on the seat next to Gloria and I saw Cathy's jaw tighten. I ordered a drink and then I led Gloria out onto the dance floor.

As I took her in my arms and started dancing she said, "I wondered what you would do."

"It was a no brainer. A choice between a girl I want to get to know better and a married woman looking for a thrill is really no choice at all."

"Oh? And just how much better do you want to know me?"

"The question is how much better do you want me to know you?"

"I'll need to give that some thought, won't I?"

Back at the table I pretty much ignored Cathy and maybe a half-hour went by. Then Gloria got up to use the ladies room and Cathy got up, came over to me and said, "Come on Rob, dance with me" and she took my arm to pull me up. I didn't want to, but I didn't want to cause a scene either so I followed her out onto the floor.

"Do you have any idea how you are making me look? It is

embarrassing."

"I'm not doing anything Cathy, you are doing it to yourself. For the last two weeks everyone has assumed that you finally came to your senses and decided that your marriage is more important than an exlover. Now you are making it look like you are chasing me. It is your imagination that people are laughing at you behind your back and if you don't get yourself under control they might actually start."

"Can we go out to your car? I need to talk to you and it needs to be private."

"I don't think so Cathy. We have taken the game as far as it needed to go."

"Please Rob, this is important to me."

I looked over at the table and Gloria was not back yet so I told Cathy I would give her five minutes. We went out to my car, got in and Cathy took a deep breath and said:

"Rob, I need, really need for you to keep on being my lover until I can end it the way I want to."

"That's what you need Cathy, but what I need is a normal relationship with a woman. I can't play games any more. Doing what you want and then going home with a case of blue balls just doesn't cut it for me."

"You don't have to go home with blue balls," she said as she unbuttoned her blouse and took it off. She wasn't wearing a brassiere and she grabbed my hands and took them up to her tits.

"I can do what you made me do the other night Rob. I promise you that if you help me you will never go home with blue balls again."

She reached for my zipper and I was so stunned and surprised that she had her hand inside my fly and on my cock before I knew what was happening. I jerked my hands away from her tits and pulled her hand out of my fly.

"Have you lost your mind? My God Cathy, you are a married woman and this was only supposed to be a game, a little fun, just something to tweak a few noses. Give it up Cathy; let it go. You did what you wanted to do. They changed the way they think of you. End it! End it now! Get your blouse back on."

I got out of the car and went back into the bar. Gloria wasn't at the table and I glanced toward the restrooms. Darla saw it and said:

"She's gone. When she found out that you went out to the parking lot with Cathy she left."

Great, I thought, just fucking great.

\*\*\*

I tried calling Gloria, but all I got was her answering machine. After nine attempts I gave up and went to bed. The next day at work I headed for Gloria's desk as soon as I walked in the door, but she saw me coming and she got up and went to the bathroom. I waited almost ten minutes, but she didn't come back so I gave up the wait and went to work. Twice more during the day I tried to see her, but she always saw me coming and managed to avoid me.

That afternoon I left work ten minutes early and when Gloria got off work she found me sitting on the hood of her car. There was an exasperated tone in her voice when she asked:

"What do you want Rob?"

"To talk to you about last night."

"I don't want to talk about last night."

"But I do Gloria. It wasn't what it looked like and I need to explain."

"You are a grown man Rob, you get to do what you want and you certainly do not need to explain it to me."

"Yes I do Gloria. It is very important to me that you don't have bad thoughts about me. Give me ten minutes and when I'm done if you tell me to piss off I'll never bother you again, but please hear me out."

"Ten minutes? Where?"

"In your car will be fine."

We got inside her car, I took a deep breath and then I told her everything that happened form the day Cathy told me there were openings where she worked right up until the previous evening (leaving out of course what Cathy had done the night before and what happened the night I lost control).

"Why are you telling me this?"

"I meant it when I said I really wanted to get to know you better. I can't do that if you aren't talking to me."

"Your step-sister. Wow. That's wild."

"Can I salvage anything out of this?"

"I don't know Rob. I'm going to have to think about it. Give me a couple of days okay?"

\*\*\*

Cathy avoided me the next two days and I suspect that it was because she was embarrassed over what she had done. On the second day Gloria asked me to meet her for breakfast before work on the following day. I was surprised when I got to the restaurant to find her sitting in a booth with Cathy. Once I had my coffee and the waitress had taken my order Gloria said:

"Okay Rob, Cathy and I have talked it over and this is how we are going to handle this."

I started to say something and Gloria held her hand up and said, "Wait until I'm done. You and I can date on the weekends, but as far as work is concerned, for the next two weeks you and Cathy will continue to have your fake affair. Near the end of the second week she will end it and I will spread the word that I overheard her telling you that she was dropping you to save her marriage. You will act down in the dumps for a while and then I will offer you a shoulder to cry on which will lead to our spending more time together and we will see where things go from there."

During this speech Cathy never looked at me and she let Gloria handle things.

"As far as the office is concerned we are already split."

"That will all be forgotten when you and Cathy stop at the bar tonight. Just act the way you did before."

"I still don't understand. As far as everyone at work is concerned it is already over between us. Why go through all this nonsense just so we can be over with again?"

"Because it is important to Cathy that it ends the way she wants it to end. That's all you need to know so humor us, okay?"

I looked at Cathy, over at Gloria and then back at Cathy. "Two weeks. Two weeks and it's over, right?"

Cathy nodded a yes and I said, "Okay. I'll give it two weeks, but then it is done whether on your terms or mine. Agreed?"

Cathy nodded a yes just as the waitress brought us our food.

***

For the next two weeks Cathy and I stopped at the bar every Tuesday and Thursday. We danced, we kissed and twice we went out to the parking lot and pretended we were having sex on the back seat of my car. The first of those Tuesdays she rubbed my bulge and whispered that she meant it when she said she would never send me home with blue balls again.

"It isn't like it hasn't already happened and it is something I do for Stan all the time."

I pushed her hand away, "It did happen Cathy and I'm sorry I was so weak, but I can't let it happen again. I can tough it out for two weeks."

On Friday, Saturday and Sunday I dated Gloria and I was beginning to think I had found my new significant other.

On the Thursday of the second week Cathy and I were eating lunch in the lunchroom with Gloria and Darla sitting at a table behind us. Cathy finished her lunch and then told me that she was ending our relationship.

"I'm sorry Rob, I really am, but I love my husband and if I keep on seeing you he will eventually find out and it would kill my marriage. I really care for you Rob and there are times I wish we had never broken up way back when. But we did break up and I met Stan. I guess I never really realized how much I loved him until it came time for me to make a choice between the two of you. I hope we can still be friends."

"We can, but no tempting me. No asking me to dance when we stop at the bar. I don't think I could handle being that close to you and not having you. Okay?"

"I think I can handle that" and she got up and left me sitting there.

By two that afternoon Gloria and Darla had made sure that everyone knew about Cathy dumping me. That night at the bar I sat and stared at my beer like a dejected man with a broken heart. I played the part of a discarded lover and finally mumbled something about being 'a wet blanket' and I got up and left.

The next night I showed up at Gloria's to pick her up for a dinner date. She invited me in, told me she wasn't quite ready yet and told me to have a seat on the couch.

"I'll be back in just a minute."

Maybe two minutes later she came back into the room wearing only high heels and nylons with a garter belt.

"I decided that we will stay in tonight. You are so gloomy over losing Cathy that you wouldn't be fun anyway. Fortunately I know that the best cure for someone's broken heart is to fuck his brains out. You want it here or in the bedroom?"

We left a trail of my clothes from the front door to her bedroom. I gently pushed her back on the bed and began licking her erect nipples. She moaned as my hand went down and rubbed her pussy and she gasped when I parted her pussy lips with a finger and found her clit. My mouth left her nipples and I licked and kissed my way down her body and she moaned as my tongue probed her belly button. I had two fingers in her pussy by then and I could feel the pressure as she pushed up at my hand. I kissed and licked my way from her navel down to her mons and then I removed my fingers and replaced them with my tongue.

"Oh God," she moaned and then she said, "I want something to play with too" and her hand found my stiff cock. She tugged on it and I knew what she wanted. I turned and moved my body so we were in the classic sixty-nine position and as I pushed my tongue deep into her she took my cock into her hot mouth.

I started working on her clit and her tongue swirled around my cock. I couldn't hold back. All of the activity with Cathy, all of the times I went home with an aching cock, had me on edge and I was ready to let go. I tried to lift off Gloria, but she grabbed me and held me as I exploded into her mouth. Again I tried to lift up, but she pulled me back and she gulped and swallowed every drop I pushed out.

I thought she would let me go as I softened, but she kept sucking and licking until I started to come alive again in the cock department. While that was going on I was attacking her pussy like a man possessed and I was rewarded by hearing her mewls of pleasure as she worked on my cock. Her hips were pushing up at my mouth and I felt that she was close. I slid a finger to her ass and I teased her rose bud. She gave a loud moan and pushed her hips hard at me and I smiled to myself as I drove my finger into her ass. She arched up from the bed and screamed and her body shook and trembled as she had a climax.

By then my cock was hard again and I went to move up between her legs. She scrambled out from under me as she said:

"No, let me do it."

She swung over me and guiding my cock with her right hand she lowered herself onto my erection. As soon as I was in her she drove herself down hard on me taking me in as deep as she could and then she started riding me. She bounced up and down on me, going higher and coming down harder with each bounce. I was trying to time my upward thrusts to meet her downward pushes. I was trying to fuck her as she was fucking me and I was getting close to coming again. I wrapped my arms around her and rolled putting her under me and then I drove into her as hard and fast as I could. She cried out as she had an orgasm and I kept pounding as I tried to reach my own.

Her heels were drumming on the backs of my legs and her nails were clawing at my back as she had another orgasm and then I felt the rush from my balls and I let go. I held myself inside her until I was limp and then I withdrew and fell to the bed beside her.

"Damn," she moaned, "It was sure enough worth the wait."

She rolled up on an elbow and looked down at me. "Have I driven the memory of losing Cathy from your mind?"

"The memory of who?"

I had my arms around her and we were cuddled up to each other and I was basking in the warm glow that comes with complete sexual satisfaction when Gloria said:

"You do know what the deal with Cathy was all about don't you?"

"From the way you ask the question I'm guessing that you already know that I don't."

"Well, it was obvious to me that big step-sister wanted an "incestuous" relationship with her little step-brother, but was having a hard time making herself do it. The fake relationship was just her way of getting you into a situation where she could make it happen, but when she got you there she couldn't bring herself to go through with it."

I was all set to say "bullshit" when I remembered Cathy taking her blouse off and reaching through my fly to grab my cock.

"I think she is past it now, but I'd watch myself around her if I were you, especially at family parties where there is a lot of drinking going on."

Then she paused a bit before saying, "Unless of course you are interested in helping the girl out. Are you?"

"Of course not," I said, not knowing if I meant it or not.

"Good," Gloria said, "I'm a one man woman and I expect my man to be a one woman man. Are you interested?"

"Do you have an application I can fill out?"

"That I do and you will be pleased to know that I do not ask for references."

"Damn! And here I am with a briefcase full of letters praising my work."

"That may be sweetie, but I am a firm believer in not taking anyone else's word for things. Speaking of firm," she said as she reached for my cock, "How we doing?"

# End of the 7<sup>th</sup> Story

# What To Do About Edie

I've been married to Edie for just a little over six years and I am constantly finding out things about her - things that I would never have expected or even believed for that matter. For instance - I just found out she is a slut.

Edie wasn't a virgin when I married her. It wasn't something that I knew first hand, but in the spirit of being up front with me Edie laid out her entire sexual history for me even to the point of naming names. I knew two of her previous lovers and she wanted to know if that was going to be a problem. The two guys were not close acquaintances, which meant that I would not normally interact with them and so I told her no. However, knowing the tendencies of males to keep on trying to fuck what you have been fucking I made a mental note to keep an eye on both of them.

Over the next couple of years, at several parties, the two of them did try more than once to hit on Edie and she always blew them off. Several others also made an attempt on my lovely bride and they also got the bums rush. As we moved into our seventh year I had no reason to believe that Edie was anything less than one hundred percent faithful. There was no doubt in my mind that she loved me and I was certainly crazy about her. The woman spoiled me rotten and I tried very hard to return the favor which made what I just found out all the more harder to understand."

As always seems to be the case I found out about Edie because I came home early one day. I was on a parts run that took me within minutes of my house and I thought that I would just swing by and have lunch with Edie. When I got home her car was in the garage, but she wasn't anywhere in the house. I figured that she must be over at the neighbors so I went into the kitchen to make myself a sandwich. Our kitchen overlooks the backyard of our neighbor to the south and I looked out the window and saw Edie in their backyard. I had told her half a dozen times not to go over there, but she never listened to me. The house was up for sale and had been vacant for almost five months. The big attraction of the place was the in ground swimming pool. The realtor had convinced Earl and Marge not to drain the pool before they moved saying that having the pool looking inviting would be a good hook for prospective buyers. When Earl and Marge lived there Edie had an open invitation to use the pool whenever she wanted. I had tried to tell her that the invitation had left town when Marge and Earl had, but as far as Edie was concerned she was going over there as long as the pool had water in it.

I had just opened the window to yell at her and tell her I was home when two men came out the back door of the house and one hollered, "Hey! What are you doing back here? This is private property and you are trespassing." Edie got up off the chaise lounge and I could see the two men feasting their eyes on the body that the two Band-Aids she called a bathing suit tried to cover. She told them that she lived next door and was keeping an eye on the place for Earl and Marge. "Bullshit lady! I'm the realtor handling the place and Earl would have told me about you. I'm sick and tired of having people trespass on the property I'm trying to sell." He told the other man to keep an eye on Edie while he went out to the car to get his cell phone so he could call the police

He turned to go and Edie said, "Wait! Maybe we can work this out. My husband will kill me if I get into trouble with the police." The man said, "What do you mean by working something out?" Then Edie made my jaw drop, "I'm sure that I can find a way to convince you to leave the cops out of this" and while she was talking she was running her hands over her breasts in as blatant a suggestion as I've ever seen. I saw the realtor glance over at the second man who had hunger written all over his face and then the realtor said, "Okay honey, let's see if you mean it." He unzipped his fly and took out his cock. Edie licked her lips and said, "Oh my, that's a nice one" and then she went to her knees in front of him and took his cock in her hand. She looked up at him and smiled, "I think I'm going to like this" and she opened her mouth and took in his cock. The other man unzipped himself and moved up to where Edie could get her hands on him and she started stroking him while sucking on the realtor.

I couldn't believe what I was seeing. My wife sucking off one stranger while jacking off another and she hadn't even put up a fight. She had just offered herself up as if it was the most natural thing in the world for her to do. That made me begin to wonder if maybe it was. After all, how did I really know that she turned aside all the passes made at her?

The realtor told the other man to go and get the chaise lounge and move it into the shade, "I'm going to cum in her mouth and then we are going to fuck the little slut." While the man moved the lounger Edie stood up and pulled off her bikini bottoms and when the lounger was in place she told the realtor to sit down on it and then she bent at the waist and took him back in her mouth. She spread her legs apart in an open invitation to the other man and he moved up behind her. He gave Edie a playful slap on the ass and then he began working his dick into her. Edie moaned around the cock in her mouth and the two men smiled ear to ear as they took Edie from both ends.

I don't remember at what point I took out my own cock, in fact I was kind of surprised to find it in my hand, but I found that I was beating myself off in time with the guy fucking Edie from behind. The realtor said, "God that's good honey, you can trespass over here any time you want as long as you are willing to keep doing this." Edie took her mouth off him long enough to say "Promise?" The realtor said, "As long as you suck my cock honey, I promise." Edie giggled and said, "I'm over here every day the sun shines sugar. Think you could handle it?" Then she went back to sucking his dick.

I watched as the three of them thrust and pushed and then I heard the realtor say, "Here it comes honey" and his hips arched up off the lounger to bury his cock deep in her throat. He must have had a lot of cum stored up because even though Edie gulped and swallowed some still leaked out of the corner of her mouth. Meanwhile the man in her pussy was pumping faster and Edie's moans began to get louder. Her mouth was still locked onto the realtor's cock as she tried to get every last drop out of him and just as the man fucking her grunted to signal that he too was emptying himself, Edie let the realtor's limp cock fall from her mouth and she gave the sharp little cry that signaled that her own climax had arrived. The man moved away from her and then both men looked at each other as if to say, "What do we do now?"

Edie looked like some sort of sex goddess propped up on the lounge chair and with cum running down the inside of her leg. With her bikini panties lying at her feet and her tits swaying her body was just crying out, "Fuck me, fuck me, somebody please fuck me." This was not the woman that I knew, the woman I had married; I did not know the woman I was watching. The surprises kept on coming, "This concrete is hard on my feet," Edie said, "Can we take this to my house where we can get more comfortable?"

I was fucked if they went around to the front of the house. Edie would see the company truck and know I was home and I couldn't get to the front of the house in time to get in my truck and leave. I wasn't ready to confront the cheating bitch just yet - I wanted to find out more about what she had been up to first - but if she came in the front door it would be all over. Luckily she headed toward the side door of the garage. I tossed my sandwich into the garbage, grabbed a dishrag and wiped up the puddle of cum I'd left on the floor and then hurried into the bedroom. I got into the closet and waited to see what would happen next.

Edie came into the room followed by the two men and she went straight to the bed and pulled off the covers. She turned to the men and said, "By the way my name is Edie. Would you like to tell me your names or would you rather just be known as mystery meat." The realtor grinned and said, "I'm Dan and this is Jim. Jim is a prospective buyer for the house next door. What do you think Jim, could you handle living next door to this sexpot?" Jim smiled, "I sure could, but my wife would be watching me like a hawk and getting over here would be a problem." Edie laughed, "When you can make it the welcome mat is always out." For the next two hours the two of them fucked Edie, she sucked their cocks and she even gave both of them her ass. The phone rang a couple of times while Edie was bouncing on the bed, but she ignored it. At one point Jim left the room to take a piss and Edie, who was sucking Dan's cock, took her mouth off him long enough to say, "If he doesn't buy the house make sure you call me when you bring the next prospect. Maybe I can help you close the sale" and then she giggled, "And you don't even have to pay me commission."

The time came when she told them they would have to leave. "I've got sheets to change and then I have to clean myself up and start dinner for my hubby." Dan asked, "Does he know you do this sort of thing?"

"Oh God no. If he knew he would probably kill me so let's just keep this as our little secret, okay?"

The two men said they would let themselves out and I got ready to get out of the house when Edie took her shower. But Edie didn't take a shower. She took a large dildo out of the bedside table drawer, leaned back against the headboard and began to fuck herself with it. I'd never seen her do that before and my dick got hard all over again. I couldn't believe it! She had just spent over two hours fucking two guys and she still wanted more. It took her several minutes to bring herself to a climax and then she licked the dildo clean and put it away. Then she picked up the phone and punched in a number, waited and then said, "Hi Bonnie (her best friend), it's me. I guess you've noticed that I'm not there. (silence and then a giggle) Oh, I guess that you could say that something came up. A couple of something's in fact." She then proceeded to tell Bonnie what had happened along with mentioning that if she were lucky it would happen again. "Who's there?" (silence) "Oh, I guess that it's a good thing that I didn't come over today." (silence) "Because Bonnie, you know I don't like fucking guys that know Jerry." (silence) "Well I haven't, not since I fucked Marvin. After I fucked him every time he was around Jerry he got one of those "I know something you don't know" smirks on his face. Harry and Joe did it to. From now on I'm not fucking anybody who knows Jerry. (silence) "No Bonnie, I will not give them blow jobs." (silence) "No I don't feel sorry for you. I've seen you handle six all by yourself before." (silence) "Okay, I'll call you tomorrow."

She hung up the phone, got off the bed and headed for the closet, but at the last second she turned and went into the bathroom. As soon as I heard the shower running I got out of the closet and out of the house.

As I drove away from the house I had a lot to think about. First, I was going to have to come up with an excuse for my boss for being gone so long. I was going to have to reevaluate my friendships with Marvin, Harry and Joe and then I was going to have to figure out what to do about Edie.

# End of the 8<sup>th</sup> Story

# Frank, Beth Ann and Glenda

I had been married to Beth Anne for eleven years when the event that started this tale took place. We had gotten together in the tenth grade, started going steady just before the start of summer vacation between eleventh and twelfth grades and were joined at the hip from then on.

We made plans to be married when we graduated from college and one month after that momentous event we tied the knot. Altogether we had been a couple for just a little over eighteen years.

We both wanted to succeed in our careers and we made the decision not to ever have children much to the despair of both sets of parents. To eliminate the need for condoms, birth control pills and the like I had myself snipped.

We both did well in our careers and after living in an apartment for nine years we finally saved up enough money for a sizeable down payment on a nice house in a good neighborhood. Our neighbors were a mix of young couples like ourselves and older more established couples. It wasn't long before we were part of the social fabric of the neighborhood. There were backyard barbecues, card nights, dinner parties and occasionally a group of us would go out for a night on the town.

Strangely, given the number of couples our own age, the couple we were closest to was in their mid-forties. Jason and Glenda were our next door neighbors and for all practical purposes you might as well have said that we somewhat lived together. There was no fence between us and our backyards blended together.

We had a six person hot tub on our patio and they had an in ground swimming pool. We both had barbecue grills and the four of us moved back and forth at will. It was not uncommon for me to come home from work and find Jase and Glennie in our hot tub or for them to look out their kitchen window and find me and Beth splashing around in their pool. Many were the times I would arrive home from a hard day at the office and find Beth, Glennie and Jase fixing dinner on our patio or theirs. It was pretty much like family.

*** 

Jason was about six two and one eighty-five and had a lean athletic body which he kept trim by using the gym he had set up in his basement. Glenda was a beautiful woman who at forty-four had a body that a woman ten years younger would have killed for. She also kept herself in shape using the gym in their basement. While Glenda was not an out and out exhibitionist she would regularly wear tight clothes, short skirts and dresses and skimpy bikinis. I would be lying if I said that being around Glenda didn't make me hard.

As what usually happens in a close knit group there is a lot of joking around and harmless flirting, but to be honest here it was mostly Glennie flirting with me. When you are as close as we were to the Carlsons (Jase and Glennie) you learn things about them and they learn things about you. One of the things that Glennie learned about me was that I liked to see sexy lingerie on ladies and that high heels and stockings were a turn on for me. She also learned that Beth didn't care for either of those things. Beth thought sexy lingerie was frivolous and a waste of money and she didn't like high heels at all. She said anything more than a two inch heel made her ankles hurt and swell.

Often when Beth and Jason weren't around or watching she would say things like "If I were your woman I'd never wear anything other than sexy under things" or "Maybe I should buy a pair of six inch stilettos and wear them for you." On a couple of occasions she pulled up the hem of her skirt or dress and gave me a quick glimpse of a thong or a pair of lacy panties.

I enjoyed Glennie's flirting and attention, but I had never considered it to be serious. I assumed that she was happy in her marriage as I was in mine and that her flirting, risqué as it was, was harmless.

*\*\**

The event that prompted this little tale happened on a Saturday at a barbecue at Glenda's and Jason's. Half the neighborhood was there and about two hours into the party I had to take a leak. I went into the house and found that both bathrooms were already occupied. I needed to go so bad that I was holding my crotch and rocking back and forth on my feet. I suppose I could have run for home, but I didn't think I could hold it that long. As familiar as I was with the Carlson's house I knew there was a toilet just off the bathroom in their master bedroom and I made a beeline for it.

I was shaking the last drops off of it when I heard the bedroom door open and close. Then I heard Beth say:

"Just what is so important that you had to get me up here to speak to me in private?"

"I'm horny as hell and I need some of your pussy," Jason said.

"For Christ's sake Jason; Frank and Glenda are just downstairs. Besides, I gave you two hours at lunch yesterday."

"Two hours on a long lunch isn't enough. I need it. Please?"

"Okay, but just a quickie. No blow job or ass. Just a quick fuck. Go lock the door while I get my panties off."

From where I was at the toilet I could see the large mirror above the counter with the two sinks and it showed me what was going on in the bedroom. Beth was wearing a skirt and she lifted it and took her panties off while Jason locked the door. Beth tossed her panties on the bed and leaned forward on her elbows and Jason unzipped, took out his cock and took Beth from behind.

I was stunned at first and then I shook it off and was just getting ready to storm into the bedroom when a voice in my head said, "Hold on. See what else happens. There might be stuff you need to know. I held myself back and then watched the action in the mirror. It was indeed a quickie as it was over in three or four minutes and then Jason pulled out. Beth stood up and grabbed her panties and at that point I figured that she would come into the bathroom and find out she was busted. That didn't happen. She wiped herself with the panties and put them on as Jason said:

"Can we get together tomorrow?"

"No. Frank and I are going to his parent's house for a birthday party."

"Monday then?"

"You know better. Mondays and Thursdays belong to Julius. You will have to wait until Tuesday," she said as she opened the door and looked to see if it was clear to leave and then the two of them left.

I stood there as things rolled around in my mind. Beth was regularly fucking Jason and from what I'd just heard she was also regularly fucking her boss? Julius Barko owned the company where Beth worked. I gave the two cheating fucks time to get clear and then rejoined the party.

As I walked out onto the patio I saw Beth talking to Glenda and I wondered if Glennie had any inkling that Jason was cheating on her and with the cunt she was talking to. No way of knowing without asking and I wasn't ready for that just yet.

Ever since leaving the bathroom my mind had been working overtime on what to do with my new found knowledge. One thing was sure. Beth and I were done. What I had to do was figure out how I wanted things to end. .

∗∗∗

Around ten the party began to wind down and Beth and I went home. When Beth was drinking, and she'd had more than a few at the barbecue, she got amorous and I expected that she was going to want to play when we went to bed.

Our love making usually started with me going down on Beth, but it wasn't going to happen on that night. It pissed me off greatly that the cunt cheated on me, but I was even more pissed that the cunt thought so little of me that she would feed me her lover's deposit. She hadn't cleaned up when she finished with Jason and she had immediately stripped, got on the bed, spread her legs and waited for me when we got to the bedroom.

Nosireebob!! Not gonna happen!

I knew that she had probably done it to me before and I hadn't noticed, but that was water over the dam and nothing I could do about it now. I'd fuck the cunt, but no fucking oral unless she wanted to try and get me up for a second time. I'd fuck the cunt because not to do so wouldn't be natural and might make her wonder why and I didn't want that. When what I was planning happened I didn't want her to see it coming.

I climbed on the bed and as I moved between the cunt's legs she reached down and pulled her cunt lips apart for my tongue, but I moved forward, pointed my cock at her hole and then shoved it home. I knew I was getting sloppy seconds, but it wasn't the first time. Not counting the times I'd followed Jason or Julius into her (unknowingly) I'd had plenty of sloppy seconds, thirds, fourths and even fifths in college at frat parties and I already knew that it wouldn't kill me. My attitude toward Beth from then on was going to be "Pussy is pussy and take it while you can get it."

I fucked her and when I finished I rolled off of her and onto my back. She sat up and said, "You aren't done yet lover" and she moved to take me in her mouth. As she sucked on my cock and tasted the mixture of mine and Jason's cum that was on it I wondered if she could differentiate tastes. Could she tell the difference between my sperm and Jason's? And how about what she got from Julius? Or for that matter a mixture of all three? I had that thought because I wouldn't have put it past her that she'd had all three on the same day a time or two.

Whatever! She did get me up again and I did fuck her a second time and then I rolled over and went to sleep.

***

I treated Sunday as any other Sunday and worked in the yard while Beth did laundry and cleaned the breakfast dishes. I was pulling weeds out of the flower beds when Beth came out in her bikini and went next door and jumped in the pool. About five minutes later Jason came out and jumped into the pool with her.

I doubted that they would do anything other than talk and maybe laugh at pulling the wool over my eyes since Glenda could show up at any time. They knew they didn't have to worry about me because I had a list of chores that I had to get done before we went to my parent's house to celebrate my mom's fiftieth birthday.

I finished my chores and went into the house to shower and got dressed and as I was dressing Beth came in and showered. As she dressed, Beth said she had a great time in the pool and was glad that we had the use of it and that it was too bad I had so much to do that I couldn't join them. I said she didn't need me there since she had Jason and Glenda to keep her company.

"Glennie went shopping. She asked me to go with her, but I just wanted a lazy day so I begged off."

"Great!" I thought. "Sloppy seconds for Frank again tonight."

There was no doubt at all in my mind that with Glenda gone and them knowing I wouldn't be coming over, they had gotten it on.

The evening at my parent's was your typical family get together and when it was over we went on home and went to bed. We undressed and Beth lay down and spread her legs for me. I knew she was expecting me to muff dive, but what she didn't know was that my pussy eating days were over as far as she was concerned. Regardless of my suspicions she might not even have fucked Jason that day, but it didn't matter because I was done doing oral on the faithless cunt.

I did fuck her and when I was done I rolled over and fell asleep even though Beth indicated she wanted to go a second time.

\*\*\*

I left for work early in the morning because I wanted to spend some personal time on the computer. I did some searching and by the time I needed to buckle down and get to work I had the names and phone numbers of several investigative agencies and divorce attorneys.

Just before lunch time I went down to the legal department and showed Stan my list of attorneys and asked for a recommendation. Stan looked over my list and told me Martin Castle would be my best bet. I then went across the hall to Security and asked Bill to take a look at my list of investigative agencies and he told me the Phoenix Investigative Service was who I should use and he told me he had a friend that worked there and said if I would like he would put me in touch. I said yes and he picked up the phone, made a call and just like that I had an appointment.

Monday night Beth made no move to initiate sex and I figured she must have gotten enough from Julius earlier in the day.

Tuesday I met with Alex Breastly at the Phoenix offices, discussed my problem and gave them a retainer. I left the Phoenix offices and went to my appointment with Martin Castle. I told him what the situation was and that I had put Phoenix on the case. He said he would get started on the paperwork right away.

That evening when I got home I faked a cough until it was bed time. When we went up to bed Beth indicated she wanted to make love which made me wonder just what it was that she was doing. She had screwed Julius Monday, but hadn't tried to give me his leftovers, but on Tuesday she was than willing to give me Jason's. I thought back over the last couple of weeks and I recognized a pattern. She never wanted to make love on the days she fucked Julius, but every other night she was ready to go (not that we did fuck on all those nights). Anyway, when I made no move to go down on Beth she asked me if something was wrong and when I said no she said:

"You haven't done oral on me since some time last week and that isn't like you."

"I've been coming down with a sore throat (and I coughed for effect) and I don't want to take a chance on making it worse. That's also why I haven't kissed you lately. I don't want to give what I might have to you. I don't even want to chance coughing in your face" I said as I pulled her into doggie position.

I fucked her hard and after I got my nut I settled onto my side of the bed expecting to go to sleep. Beth had other ideas. She fondled my soft cock until she was able to get me hard again (with a little help from her mouth) and I fucked her doggie for the second time that night. As I pounded into her I wondered if Beth had become a nymphomaniac. Between Julius, Jason and me she was getting fucked almost daily and always seemed to want more.

I finished the second time and told Beth I was bushed and I needed to get some rest since I had a busy day in front of me Wednesday. She pouted some, but gave up on trying to get a third time out of me.

\*\*\*

The rest of the week went by and I did my best to act normal around Beth. We had sex every night but Mondays and Thursday which I already knew belonged to Julius and I still wondered why she wouldn't fuck me on the days she did Julius. I knew when I was following Jason into her because now that I knew what was going on I could pick up the signs. Before my discovery while in Jason's and Glenda's bathroom I had always believed Beth when she told me she was wet because she was horny and couldn't wait to get home to me and make love. As much as we fucked why wouldn't I believe it? Now I knew that she was wet because someone else was there before me. Then there was also the fact that Beth, in thinking that she had me so snowed I wouldn't notice anything, didn't take elementary precautions like pushing her cum stained panties under the rest of the dirty clothes, but instead just dropped them in on top.

I managed to get through the weekend without giving Beth and indication that I was onto her. I'd kept a close eye on her and she was never able to get away from me on those two days so I knew that she hadn't been able to spread for Jason. Knowing that I did go down on her Sunday night for what I figured was going to be the last time.

\*\*\*

Monday Beth didn't want to play and her panties in the dirty clothes hamper told me that Julius had gotten his. Tuesday morning I got the call from Phoenix and made an appointment to see them on Wednesday. That night was amorous and I fucked her knowing that it was going to be the last time because she was going to be out of the house by the weekend.

There were no surprises on Wednesday since I already knew what the Phoenix operatives were going to find. The report showed her going to a motel on Mondays and Thursdays with Julius and a different motel on Tuesdays and Fridays with Jason. It was noticed that Julius and Beth always used the same motel so the Phoenix people had bribed the desk clerk and ended up with audio and video of Beth and Julius. They did the same thing at the motel that Jason and Beth used.

"It is all on the CDs" I was told when they were handed to me. "It won't be admissible in court, but it is proof positive and that is what you wanted."

I thanked the man and left his office. I went back to the attorney and told him I'd give him a call and tell him what time and where. I went home and copied the parts with Julius onto one CD and the parts with Jason on another. Then I copied some of the stills made of Julius and Beth onto paper and I was set to go.

On Thursday I called Julius and asked him if he could meet me for lunch. I told him that I was planning a surprise for Beth and that I would like his help in setting it up. I knew that Thursday was the day he spent the lunch hour fucking Beth so I was not surprised when he said he has a previous engagement that he couldn't get out of. He asked me if Friday would work and I said that it would.

I knew he would be fucking Beth and what I wanted to do was plant "I wonder what he wants" in his mind so he would think about it for the next twenty-four hours. There was a chance he might tell Beth, but it wouldn't matter. All it would do is make her curious as to what I was going to do. She wouldn't mention it when she comes home that evening because she would want me to think she was surprised. At least that is what I was gambling on.

The evening I attempted to have sex with Beth even though I knew she never gave me any on the days she fucked Julius. I wasn't at all surprised when she said she was too tired, but I had hoped for one more fuck before I dropped the hammer on her.

***

Friday morning on my way out the door I kissed Beth goodbye and smiled to myself at knowing that it was two things. It was the last kiss she would ever get from me and I was not only kissing her goodbye as I left for work, but I was also kissing our marriage and her goodbye forever.

At noon I met with Julius at Tricocci's for lunch and after we had ordered Julius asked:

"Just what is this surprise you are setting up for Beth and how can I help out?"

"I'm going to hit her with divorce papers and I need your help in deciding how to do it."

"You have to be shitting me! You want my help in having her served?"

"No. What I want is for you to decide whether I have her served with papers that list Irreconcilable Differences as the reason for the divorce or papers that list Adultery as the cause" and as I was saying that I slid a folder across the table to him. "Take a look at what is in the folder and it will all become clear to you."

He opened the folder and looked at the four 8x10 photos and his face turned pale.

"This is the way it is going to go Jules baby," I said. "This is a no fault state so regardless of how I file Beth and I have to split everything fifty-fifty. That means that I'll have to sell the house and give her half of the proceeds. The problem is that I love that house and I don't want to give it up. That means in order for me to keep it I'll have to come up with Beth's share and I don't have it.

"That's where you come in. I'm going to need two things from you. I had the house appraised and given our equity I'm going to have to come up with 25 thousand to buy out Beth's half. So the first thing I need from you is a certified check for that amount. The second thing I need for you to do is give Beth a two hundred dollar a week raise so that our incomes are equal and I won't have to pay alimony."

"You are out of your fucking mind if you think I'm going to do that!"

"Your choice of course, but this is the way I see it. You do the two things I've asked of you and I file under irreconcilable differences, the divorce goes through, and I live happily ever after. You don't do the two things I want and adultery is the way I will go and since this is one of the states that allow it I will have you served in your office for alienation of affections. Then I will send everything I have on you and Beth to your wife. Remember the fifty-fifty part? Half of everything you own, including your business will go to your wife if she decides to go for a divorce. Want to risk it?

"The papers will be served today, but you get to decide which papers will be served. You have just a little over an hour and a half to make that decision. I need your certified check in hand by two o'clock and if I don't have what I've asked for by two o'clock at one minute after two I'll call my attorney and tell him to go the adultery route and as soon as I'm done speaking with him I will call a messenger service and have a package on the way to your wife."

I got up and walked out without even touching what I had ordered for lunch. And stuck Julius with the tab. I went back to my office and got back to work.

I wasn't at all surprised when at one-forty a woman wearing a shirt that said Quicksilver Messenger Service on it came to my office and had me sign for an envelope. I opened it and found a cashier's check for 25 thousand. I picked up the phone and called the attorney and told him to have Beth served with the irreconcilable difference paperwork when she got off work at five.

I left work early to make sure that I got home before Beth. I was not surprised when my cell went off at five minutes after five and the display showed that it was Beth. I let it go to voice mail. I was somewhat surprised that I didn't get the call earlier. I half expected Julius to go back to work and tell Beth that they had been busted and that she would try to get in touch with me and tell me not to do anything rash before we could talk things over. I guess Julius kept quiet about it.

*** 

When Beth walked in the front door at five thirty-five the first thing she saw was three suitcases and five trash bags on the floor just inside the door. I was in the living room watching the early news on TV and having a beer when she came into the room spouting:

"What the hell is with this divorce bullshit?!"

"No bullshit Beth, I'm cutting you loose."

"I don't know what your damned problem is Frank, but whatever it is we can fix it and there is no need for you to move out."

"Tell me something Beth. Can you un-fuck Julius? Can you make it so that your Mondays and Thursdays at the Motel 6 never happened? And I'm not moving out, you are."

Her face went ashen when I hit her with the information and I went on:

"I filed using irreconcilable differences so as to keep things quiet. No one other than you, me and Julius need to know that you are a cheating cunt and we can keep things low key as long as you sign the paperwork and move out."

I got up off of the couch and went over and pushed the 'play' button on the VCR and on the TV screen Beth saw Julius fucking her in her butt.

"You don't really want me to change my filing to adultery do you? You don't really want me to go public with this do you? Can you imagine what your mother's reaction would be if she saw this? How about the rest of your friends and relatives? You are going to need your job Beth. No matter which way I file you are going to need a job. Do you think you will still have one if I get a copy of this to Julius's wife?

"Your choice of course. It doesn't matter to me which way it goes as long as it goes. We have nothing to talk about Beth. I don't want to know why, when or how it started. I don't want to hear you say you are sorry, that it was only sex and that you love only me. All I want to hear is the closing of the door behind you when you leave. So just take your stuff, put it in your car and go."

"That's it? Eighteen years down the toilet just like that?"

"You're the one who pushed the lever down to flush things Beth, not me."

I ejected the tape from the player and handed it to Beth. "Your copy Beth. Don't worry; I have plenty more if I need to send them out."

I went into the kitchen, got another beer and went out into the garage to putter around and kill time. Through the garage door window I watched Beth load her car with the suitcases and garbage bags full of clothes. Once loaded she got in the car, backed down the drive and was gone.

*** 

During all of the actions I took in setting up the divorce I'd deliberately kept Jason out of things. I had a different scenario in mind for him. Quite frankly, since he had fucked my wife I was planning on trying to fuck his behind his back just as he had fucked mine behind my back.

I found things to do away from the house over the weekend and I didn't see Jason or Glenda until Sunday evening. I was sitting in the hot tub sipping a beer when they both came over to join me.

"I haven't seen Beth all weekend," Glenda said.

"Beth doesn't live here anymore."

"She doesn't? Why? What happened?"

"I caught her cheating on me and I kicked her out."

I was looking at Jason's face when I said that and I saw fear come over it as Glenda said:

"I find that hard to believe. You two were so perfect together."

"I thought that too until I got an anonymous email asking if I had any idea what Beth was doing on her lunch hour every Monday and Thursday. I checked it out and found that she was having long lunches with her boss at the Motel 6."

"You must have been crushed."

"I was. I thought we had something good going, but I guess I was just wearing rose colored glasses."

"So what are you going to do?"

"I filed for divorce and now I just need to go on with my life."

"Well Jase and I are here for you."

"Thanks. It is good to have such great friends" and I was looking at Jason when I said it and he gave me a weak smile.

\*\*\*

I wasn't going to take an outright shot at Glenda. My plan was to let her adjust to the absence of Beth and then when she started flirting with me again I would start flirting back and see where I could take it.

I expected that Glenda would tone it down figuring that I was despondent over my failed marriage and she would wait a bit before going back to flirting with me, but I was wrong. Glenda became more obvious in her flirting almost immediately. Friendly kisses that were just a shade away from being passionate, a lot touching, and even some footsie playing under the table.

On a Thursday night two weeks after Beth moved out I was sitting in the hot tub and Glenda came over and got in the tub with me. She had on one of her skimpiest bikinis and I got an instant hard on. Glenda could see it when she looked down at the water and I thought I detected a bit of a smile appear on her face.

"How you doing?" she asked.

"So so."

"Got any plans for this weekend?"

"I'm supposed to go to a cocktail party hosted by one of my clients, but I'm trying to figure a way to get out of it."

"Why?"

"It's one of those things where you will stick out like a sore thumb if you show up alone."

"Would you go if you had a date?"

"Sure."

"Okay then; what time are we leaving?"

"What?"

"Jase is out of town and won't be back until sometime Monday so I'm free for the weekend."

She paused for a second and then said, "Unless you would be ashamed to be seen with me."

"Don't be stupid Glennie. I'd love to have you with me. Every man there will envy me and I'll probably end up having to fight to keep you with me."

"Well aren't you the silver tongued devil."

She leaned toward me and kissed me on the lips and I poked my tongue at her lips and she gave me a surprised look. She got up to get out of the tub and said:

"I need to dig through my closet to find something suitable to wear." Then she smiled and said, "You want me to wear stockings and heels for you?"

"Of course I would."

She laughed and said, "You got it" and went on home.

As I watched her go I as naturally thinking that with Jason out of town it might be a good time to raise the level of flirting to see what might happen.

***

I picked Glenda up at six-thirty and when she opened the door to me my eyes almost popped out of my head. Glenda was wearing a very elegant little black cocktail dress and four inch 'come fuck me' pumps. She looked both sexy and classy at the same time. She was a walking wet dream!

I saw her glance down at my obvious erection and smile. In the car the little black dress rode up exposing a lot more leg and I saw that the nylons she was wearing were thigh highs and I kept glancing over at the sight and Glenda beamed. She knew damned well what she was doing to me and she liked it.

At the party I introduced Glenda as my girlfriend and we spent the night sipping champagne and socializing. Glenda received quite a few admiring glances and one guy I knew asked me where in the world had I found her and if she had a sister.

At eleven things started breaking up. Glenda's intentions were obvious when she said:

"I've had enough champagne. Why don't we just go back to your place for a nightcap or two?"

When we got to the house I went into the kitchen to build a couple of drinks and when I carried them back into the living room I found Glenda sitting on the couch and she was naked except for her nylons and high heels. I took in the sight as I handed her the drink and said:

"This is a surprise."

"Why?" she said as she took the drink. "I've done just about everything except flat out ask you to fuck me since the day you moved in."

She took a sip from her drink, set the glass down, then went to her knees in front of me, unzipped my fly, eased my stiff cock out into the open and then proceeded to give me the best head I'd ever gotten. She swallowed hungrily when I came and then stood up and took both of my hands and carried them up to her tits.

"Pinch my nipples Frank. Tug on them, squeeze them; it excites me."

I did what she asked. I pinched them, tugged on them and rolled them between my fingers. I dropped my right hand down and rubbed her pussy. I found her clit and massaged it. She whimpered and in a throaty voice said:

"Fuck me Frank. Please fuck me."

I was surprised when I discovered the nasty kinky side of Glenda. As I laid her down on the couch and eased my cock into her incredibly tight shaved pussy (I found out later she had shaved especially for the night). She had always appeared to be a classy, elegant and refined lady so it came as a surprise when I learned that Glenda liked talking dirty and being talked dirty to and she liked her sex hard and rough.

Using words like fuck, cock, cunt and slut some of the things she said that night were:

"That's it Frank; fuck me harder."

"Don't hold back damn it; fuck me, fuck me."

"Oh yeah, that's it Frank; fuck me and make me your bitch."

"Treat me like a dirty whore Frank; fuck me, fuck me, fuck me."

"Don't pull out Frank. Cum inside me. Fill my hungry cheating cunt."

Replying in kind I called her a bitch, a dirty old slut, a cheating cunt and I told her that I was going to use her as a cum dump.

After the first fuck on the couch we moved to the bedroom. I fucked her four times that night and after each time Glenda would take me in her mouth and suck on me until I was hard again. We did it missionary, doggie and cowgirl. The highlight of the night for me was when Glenda told me she had never been fucked in the ass and was more than willing to let me take her anal cherry. I of course took her up on the invitation.

After I came in her ass, she tried to get met me up for another go (after washing my dick first) but she just couldn't get the job done. We fell asleep cuddled up with each other.

\*\*\*

I woke up in the morning and disentangled myself from Glenda who was still sound asleep and headed for the shower. I was washing my hair when the shower curtain was pushed aside and Glenda climbed into the shower with me. I washed her back and she washed my front with predictable results. We ended up back in bed and fucked twice – the second time up her butt – and then we showered again and headed out for breakfast at the Village Inn.

Sitting across from each other Glenda said, "You seem surprised about last night."

"Of course I was. You have always flirted with me and I thought that is all it was ever meant to be."

"The truth is I have wanted to have you almost from the very day you moved in next door to us, but I thought that you were too into Beth to take me up on my obvious hints."

"Why? I thought you and Jason were solid."

"Jason is an asshole. He started cheating on me before the ink was dry on our marriage license and I've always wanted to pay him back in kind, but I never found anyone that I wanted to do it with until I met you. Quite frankly I expected you to take me up on my flirting a long time ago."

"Why would you expect that?"

"I thought you might want to get even with Jason because he was fucking Beth."

"You knew?"

"He started fucking her three weeks after you moved in."

"You have to be kidding me. It started two years ago?"

"Yep."

"Now I feel like an idiot. I didn't find out until a few weeks ago. Two years and I didn't have the foggiest. Why are you still with him if he has been cheating on you as long as he has?"

"I didn't find out what he had been doing until we had been married three years. By the time I found out I was settled into a lifestyle that I didn't want to give up. Jason hasn't a clue that I know what he has been doing, but I do know and because I know I plan on keeping you in my pussy for as long as you want me to."

"I still don't understand, why me? I would have thought you would have started to get even with him a long time ago."

"For a long time I never had the nerve and when I finally got it I decided not to do it until I met someone worth losing my marriage over. Enter you."

"Worth losing your marriage over? I'm worth losing your marriage over?"

"If we were found out and I had to split from Jason you would take me in, wouldn't you?"

"In a heartbeat sweetie; in a fucking heart beat!"

Glenda stayed with me all weekend only leaving me to go home an hour before Jason's flight was due to arrive.

The only down side to the weekend was that I was just a little pissed at Glenda for not telling me about Jason and Beth. Pissed, but not enough not to let her fuck my brains out.

\*\*\*

For the next year Glenda and I got it on every chance we got. Glennie loved the fact that she was having an affair with a younger man. It made her feel sexy that a man ten years younger than she was wanted her and she was more than happy to do anything she could to keep me happy.

While Glennie was keeping me happy my divorce skated through. Beth signed off on everything and we split everything fifty/fifty and I used the money I got from Julius to buy her out of her part of the house and then she dropped out of sight and I never saw or heard from her again.

One weekend while Jason was attending a golf outing at a golf course somewhere in California, Glenda and I spent from six p.m. Friday until three p.m. Sunday doing our best to fuck each other into exhaustion. Before I left to go next door to my place Glenda asked:

"Do you think you could stand living with me?"

"Silly question sweetie. You can move in with me today. We can have you packed and out of here before Jason's plane lands."

"I'm not thinking of anything that quick. I've decided to divorce Jason. The only thing I'll hate about it is losing this house. It will have to be sold for the asset split."

"No problem sweetie. I'll lend you the money to buy him out. You keep the house and when your divorce is final I'll sell my house, marry you and move in with you."

"You would do that?"

"I said it once before and I'll say it again. In a heartbeat sweetie; in a fucking heartbeat."

And that's just what happened. Glenda had collected a lot of information on Jason over the years and she gave him a choice much as I had given Julius a choice. Irreconcilable Differences or Adultery and Jason chose not to go the adultery route.

The day Glenda filed I put my house up for sale and I sold it and closed on the deal right about the time Glennie's divorce became final. A week after her divorce was final we were married in a civil ceremony. She put my name on the title to her house and I used some of the proceeds from the sale to put a hot tub on the patio right next to the swimming pool and used the rest to pay down her mortgage. And even though some might not believe it, we lived happily ever after.

## The End


Here is a sample from another story you may enjoy:

7 STORIES IN 1
SHE NEEDS MORE
Erotica Short Stories, Vol. 17
HOT EROTICA
JUST PLAIN BOB

Everybody has bad days, but when I have one it seems to go on forever. I was sitting on the side of the road with a flat on the right rear and when I opened the trunk I found the spare flat too. I picked up my cell phone to call Triple A for roadside assistance and found that I was in a dead spot and couldn't connect to anything. That left me with two options – walk up the road or walk down the road. No real choice there. I could see my destination sitting on top of a hill about a mile and a half away and going the other way would be a five-mile walk to reach a phone. I grabbed my bag and set out for Charlie's place.

As I trudged up the hill I thought, for at least the twentieth time, that I really didn't want to be there. I would much rather have been in my own home with my wife all to myself rather than having to share her with thirty or forty other people, especially since she had been gone almost a week. Arrington, Ari for short, was the Executive Assistant to Charles Wellington Byrns, President, CEO, and Chairman of the Board and major stockholder in one of the Midwest's largest corporations. Ari's job meant that she went where Charlie went and that was all over the place and often. I wasn't very happy about it since I would much rather have her home with me, but Ari had made it perfectly clear when I proposed that if she accepted she was keeping her job. She told me that I needed to understand that the condition was non-negotiable and that she would not entertain any motions to reopen the question after we were married. Her straightforward, no-nonsense approach to things was one of the qualities that I admired in her and if letting her keep her job was the price I had to pay to get her, so be it. Besides, I planned on using trickery – make babies and turn her into a stay at home mom. So far it hadn't happened, but I was trying hard.

Ari had been gone on a four-day trip to San Francisco and she and Charles had flown in at four that afternoon and had gone directly from the airport to his house. Tomorrow there was going to be a pool party at his house and the plan was for me to meet Ari there and spend the weekend. Then on Monday Ari and I were going to take off for a week and spend some time together where we could be alone.

I suppose the easiest thing for me to do would have been to walk to the gate and hit the buzzer and wait for Charlie or someone to come down and get me, but the gate was still a mile ahead of me and I could see the house just off to my right. I decided to go cross-country and save myself half a mile. The ground was a little rougher than I expected and it was slow going. It was getting dark as I approached the house from the side and I could see Ari sitting out on the patio reading a magazine. Charles came out of the house in a bathrobe and walked up to Ari and I was just about to shout and wave when he opened the bathrobe and put his hard cock inches from Ari's face. She put down the magazine, leaned over, and took his cock in her mouth and started sucking him off. Not a word had been said. He just walked over, stick out his cock, she opened her mouth and sucked.

At first I was stunned into immobility and I just stood there and watched. Then the anger started to build and I began moving toward the house with mayhem on my mind. But the closer I got the more I wanted to know about what was going on. I slowed my advance until I was close enough to hear Charlie say, "That's it baby, no one does it better than you."

I stopped and stood there quietly as my wife gave her boss a blowjob. I was wearing dark clothes, it had gotten dark outside and there was a stand of trees behind me. I figured if I stayed still I wouldn't be noticed. Ari was caressing Charlie's balls as she sucked his cock and his moans of pleasure masked any sound that her sucking might have made, but I was painfully aware of what those sounds were like and just as painfully aware that I was going to miss them after this night was over.

If you enjoyed this sample then look for **She Needs More**.

You may also like the books by these authors:

Ben E. Dorm

*Mrs.*
MOON

ROMANCE EROTICA

Conversation ceased when Mrs Moon entered. She paused and looked around, letting them see her as she gave the place the once over. It hadn't altered at all to her notice: ill-fitting, threadbare carpet, once blue but faded and dirtied by years of traffic, mostly scuffed and dirty work boots, all raggedy at the periphery and curled in one corner. The same old calendar hung on the wall, a bosomy young blonde smiling out, the young woman at least two years older than the year displayed in the calendar's header. A knackered settee sat against the back wall, while a remnant from some ancient kitchen stood in one corner, a freestanding unit brought in by someone to act as a surface upon which rested a kettle, a five litre bottle of water, and the makings for tea and coffee. There was a fridge next to the kitchen unit, unloved and unclean, its job being to keep milk cold during the working week as well as lager for the Friday afternoon drink-up. A low coffee table was in front of the sofa, much be-ringed by coffee and tea stains, an overflowing ashtray in its geograph-ical centre despite the no-smoking sign on display.

"Hello, Mrs Moon," one of the men said, a stocky, grey-haired man, his hair cut very short to his scalp. The man pushed himself upright from where he'd been leaning against the fridge, his arms folding across his chest as he moved. Mrs Moon knew him to be in his late forties, the foreman of the workshop.

"Tim," she replied, acknowledging the greeting. She surveyed the assembled group, eying each in turn. "Hello, boys," she breathed.

Three of the four remaining men mumbled their hellos, the trio wearing the same garb as Tim, grease-stained, baggy overalls. They were ubiquitous twenty-something's, one of whom Mrs Moon found rather attractive. The other two were nondescript, longish dark hair in need of a trim. In Mrs Moon's eyes they were unremarkable in every way, except to serve as extra meat in Mrs Moon's diet. She couldn't even recall their names – Alan and Pete or some such. Anyway, she had no interest at all in their personal lives or their circumstances. The young mechanics were always changing, with one leaving to be replaced by another, Tim being a constant in all the months Mrs Moon had enjoyed her Thursday after-noon sojourn in their company. She nodded at the trio, two of whom were sitting in the questionable embrace of the sofa, knees high because of insubstantial support in the sway-backed piece of furniture, the good-looking one sitting on the seat of an old ladder-backed chair, his arms dangling over the back support, the chair reversed beneath him.

The fifth man, the one standing with his back to the rear wall, the man in the suit, she ignored completely.

"Are you ready?" Mrs Moon asked, moving into the room with an exaggerated swing of her hips. "I hope so," she added, facing square on to the sofa, fists on her hips. "Because I'm so fucking horny…"


If you enjoyed this sample then look for **Mrs. Moon**.

# Amy Redek

*Farell*

Hot Romance Erotica

'It was a dark and stormy night and the lightening crashed and the thunder flashed,' I began before being interrupted by a bright seven-year-old girl.

'Excuse me, Mr. Farrell,' her right arm held up high, 'but shouldn't that be the lightning flashed and the thunder crashed?'

'Quite right, my young Miss. I changed the words to see if you were paying attention,' which proved that at least one was. This was becoming my party piece as I was always invited to the birthday parties of my niece and nephew and as the end of the party was nigh, I would always be asked to tell a ghost story. The floor would be cleared and we would only have the light of a solitary candle on the mantel piece behind me as the children sat in a semi-circle before me, holding hands. So in the gloom of the room with just this single flickering light that didn't show my features, I had to make the most of the story with the tones of my voice. They liked it when it was deep and sonorous to try and portray that somewhere outside of our circle was a mysterious and threatening presence. One year I didn't begin with those words and I had cries of dismay, so ever since, I've had to begin my stories the same way. They understood these words whether it be around an old house alone in the middle of the moors, or a castle perched high on a cliff edge with the seas crashing and rolling against the sharp jagged rocks that had seen many ships founder. They could imagine the single flashing light high up in the castle, luring a ship to its destruction on the rocks below.

These were pictures they could conjure up in their mind's eye as I described the wind and the way that it talks to man, bird and beast. This was the beginning to their story and it was not to be left out though the critics say that a book should never open with these lines, but it was the way that my critics who sat before me all wanted it to begin.

But my own story for you really started with it being quite the opposite, though if I ever got to tell it to the children, it would have to be different. Spring had arrived and the sun was shining and all seemed right with the world. My name is Michael Farrell and I'm slightly overweight for my height of six foot if taken with my being thirty two years of age. I have light blue eyes, clean shaven, average features and have brown to black coloured hair which is of no value to the story but just helps to fill up the picture for you to see me.

I live alone in a cottage, of which there are twelve in what is known as Meadows Lane that leads nowhere from the lane at the top. This top lane, or road is one of those nightmare thoroughfares that only has passing areas about two hundred yards apart. Not lay-bys but just bits of ground where the hedge has been crushed over the years and were now just bare patches of earth that were full of mud and icy water during the winter. Many's the time you can hear the honking of horns as two vehicles meet and neither want to reverse to clear the way. It is usually the one with a female inside that finally gives way and makes the tricky job of reversing round a blind bend to be able to pull into the hedge lined gap.

This was the road at the top of my lane and it had just a small pub and one shop that sold a lot of nothing, and to complete this part of the village, there were six cottages either side of these two public places. These were all on the right as we came out and turned left from Meadows Lane because the land opposite and onto which my cottage backed, was Meadows Farm.

It was over a quarter of a mile before we came to the stables on the right and this was directly opposite another lane that ran in the same direction as the one I lived in. Now this would show the ingenuity of the district's planning many years ago, because it bounded the other side of Meadows Farm and that my lane was called Meadows Lane, they named this one by just dropping the letter S. Brilliant thinking on someone's part. This lane too had twelve cottages and so it was almost a mirror image to mine if one could look down from above.

Now at the bottom of the two lanes and of the farm in between, was what were locally known as the cliffs. A misnomer if ever there was one like calling our hamlet a village. Our cliffs were about twenty foot high and as the land and soil slowly broke away with wind and rain, they became slopes that ran down to a narrow pebbled beach, if I could even call it that. Though the land of the farm was flat where the farmhouse stood, it rose up towards the sea end but rolled down on either side to where the lanes were, so from where I lived, I couldn't see the lane on the other side of these fields because of this small hill.

I know, I know, you're getting impatient for me to start the story but I had to give you the lay out and topography of the place first and you'll understand why in a minute. Now I'll get to the problem I caused our postie, postman to you townies, his name by the way is Pat. Well, that is what everybody calls him like they call our village Toy Town. We don't have a Noddy but we do have a Big Ears, but due to the size of the fellow, no one has ever dared call him that. Built like a brick…, er, outhouse, with arms and shoulders that many a tree would be proud to have limbs like that. He was much in demand at harvest time because he could pitch fork even the most soggiest of hay bales to toss it over twenty feet high onto the hay wagon.

But the problem I caused our postman was of my surname Farrell, because there was another man of that name in the opposite lane, only his Christian name was Nicholas. When we did eventually meet, it became Mick and Nick, mine coming first alphabetically. What compounded postman Pat's problem was none of the cottages had numbers or names and he delivered by the surname on the letter, so sometimes I got Nick's and he got mine if the writer dropped the letter S. Also I think Pat had an eye problem to tell the difference between the two letters of our Christian names.

It was a joke when it first happened as I got a letter that was meant for Nick and so I took a walk along the cliffs and over the hill to hand deliver it myself for which he opened a bottle of beer as a thank you. Then another day he delivered one to me and I reciprocated with a bottle of beer and a chat. Now this would happen three, maybe four times a year so we both now always kept a few bottles of beer available in the pantry as payment.

It was on this glorious spring morning that Pat delivered one for Nick to my cottage, so after I had my breakfast and washed up and put the things away decided to take over his letter. I put it in my jacket pocket and went out into the garden but stopped as I looked at the sorry state of my roses. I saw that they could do with a bit of nutrient about now if I wanted a good showing this year, so decided to call in at the stables first to order some manure.

I walked up my lane and turned left and gave a wave to Dave, the pub landlord as he was seeing to his weekly delivery by the draymen. I ambled along the lane, keeping one ear cocked for the sound of any approaching vehicle from either direction, but as we are such a way off the beaten track, we don't get that many. I called in at the stables and spoke to the head lad; lad? He was nearly double my age and agreed to drop a couple of bags off at my cottage though I stressed that only when there was time and not to rush, which was a bit of a joke because nobody rushed in Toy Town.

With the manure ordered, I then went down the lane to Nick's cottage and I called out as I entered the garden but only got silence as a response. I went round to his back door which was never locked and went in, calling out his name again. The kitchen was clean and tidy but still no Nick. I went and felt the tea cloth and found that it was damp which told me he'd eaten and washed up. I went to his pantry and took out a bottle of beer and put it in the middle of the table so that it was a reminder of what he owed me as I propped his letter up against it.

I went out closing the door and down through his garden for the walk along the cliffs back to my place. It certainly was a pleasure to walk through the grass and feel the first hint of warmth from the sun on my back so I took my jacket off and slung it over my shoulder, enjoying the slight breeze coming off the sea and I could hear what I thought were larks as I got near the top of the small hill.

It was by looking up into the sky and not looking where I was putting my feet that I tripped and went sprawling flat down on my stomach, and as I raised my head, came face to face with Nick. There, in the grass, eyes half closed and the mouth fixed in a rictus of a grin, a foot away from me was Nick's head…

If you enjoyed this sample then look for **Farell**.

# HIS WIFE
*and*
# HER HUSBAND
## SPOUSES WHO STRAY

HOT ROMANCE EROTICA
# JACK RYDER

Shelly and I were always sort of mismatched now that I look back at the eight years we were husband and wife. I was always a night owl. Preferring the late night hours to write my stories when there were no distractions and the rest of the neighborhood was asleep.

Shelly was one of those early to rise and early to bed sorts. She spent her morning working out to keep her highly tuned body at its peak performance. She spent the rest of her day with her clients. Shelly was a very popular personal trainer in our little part of the world.

Things went fairly well the first three or four years of our relationship. We could laugh off our differences as amusing quirks that added to the uniqueness of our love. But after a while, those differences began to grate on us. It began to erode the foundation of that uniqueness.

Shelly was always so busy that she often left things a mess. It wasn't just a little mess either. She would leave any room she'd been in looking like a tornado had roared through. After years of cleaning up after her, I began to resent it. I felt like I was her personal maid or something.

It seemed that Shelly's biggest resentment was that I would try to get sexual with her when she was ready for bed. But she grew more and more resistant as the years went by. Often telling me she was too tired or that it pissed her off that I would get back up afterward to go do some more writing.

After a while, we fell into a routine of sorts. I stopped complaining about her messiness but became very quiet and uncommunicative when she was home. She responded by coming home later and later and curtailing our sex life to a holiday treat or as a favor when she wanted something special. Those episodes usually occurred each time I received a large bonus when one of my books did very well.

I'm sort of telling you all this boring stuff so you can get an idea of how we sort of drifted our own directions. I became accustomed to doing pretty much whatever I wanted to go do. And Shelly pretty much came and went as she pleased as well.

But you need to understand that I never once considered having an affair or seeking out companionship in any manner. I truly believed that we were just suffering through growing pains and that eventually things would straighten out for us.

I also have to tell you that I have a very active sexual drive. As time passed, I found ways to…take care of my own needs so to speak. I found ways to satisfy myself. I found there were many ways that one could have anonymous sex and there were many others that were seeking the same release.

It started out with a few harmless trips to the Adult Arcade out on the edge of town. The sign had just caught my eye one afternoon after having an argument with Shelly. She had taunted me afterward saying that the next time she would fuck me is when pigs fly.

I felt a little apprehensive when I first stepped into the arcade. Afraid I might see someone that I know and they would think I was some sort of pervert. I was surprised to see that there were nearly a dozen people milling around in the large center area that was filled with rows of videos, sex toys and sexy lingerie.

I noticed a couple of men over in the back corner by the gay magazine row. They seemed to be sizing me up as they gawked at the magazines they were holding. It even appeared that two of them were sort of petting each other below the level of the shelves.

There were a couple of middle age women that seemed like they were a little embarrassed to be here. But they were whispering requests at the counter clerk.

I figured they were here to purchase some stuff to spice up their sex life at home. I felt a little jealous as I thought of that. At least these women were trying to find ways to keep their sex life alive.

I also noticed one woman in the other back corner alone. She was holding up sexy panties as if inspecting them. But she kept looking over as if to see if I was paying attention to her. She was wearing a very short mini skirt and extremely tight pull over top. The way her nipples were poking against the tight cotton fabric, it was easy to tell she was not wearing a bra. She sort of looked like a hooker.

I noticed the hall way to the arcade with the private booths. I smiled at the woman one last time then made my way down the hall. I went to the very last booth at the far end of the hall and closed the door behind me. I quickly shoved $5 in the pay slot and selected a porn video to watch.

I just got my pants down and was gently tugging on my prick when I heard the door to the booth next to mine open and close. Moments later, I heard the sound of the machine taking money in the next booth. Then I heard a loud moaning as the porn came on in the next booth. In a few seconds, the sound became the same as the video that I was watching.

I was just getting a good rhythm to my jerking when I suddenly heard "Pssssst," coming from the wall next to me. When I glanced down, I saw a four inch hole in the wall at just the same level as my cock…

If you enjoyed this sample then look for **His Wife And Her Husband**.

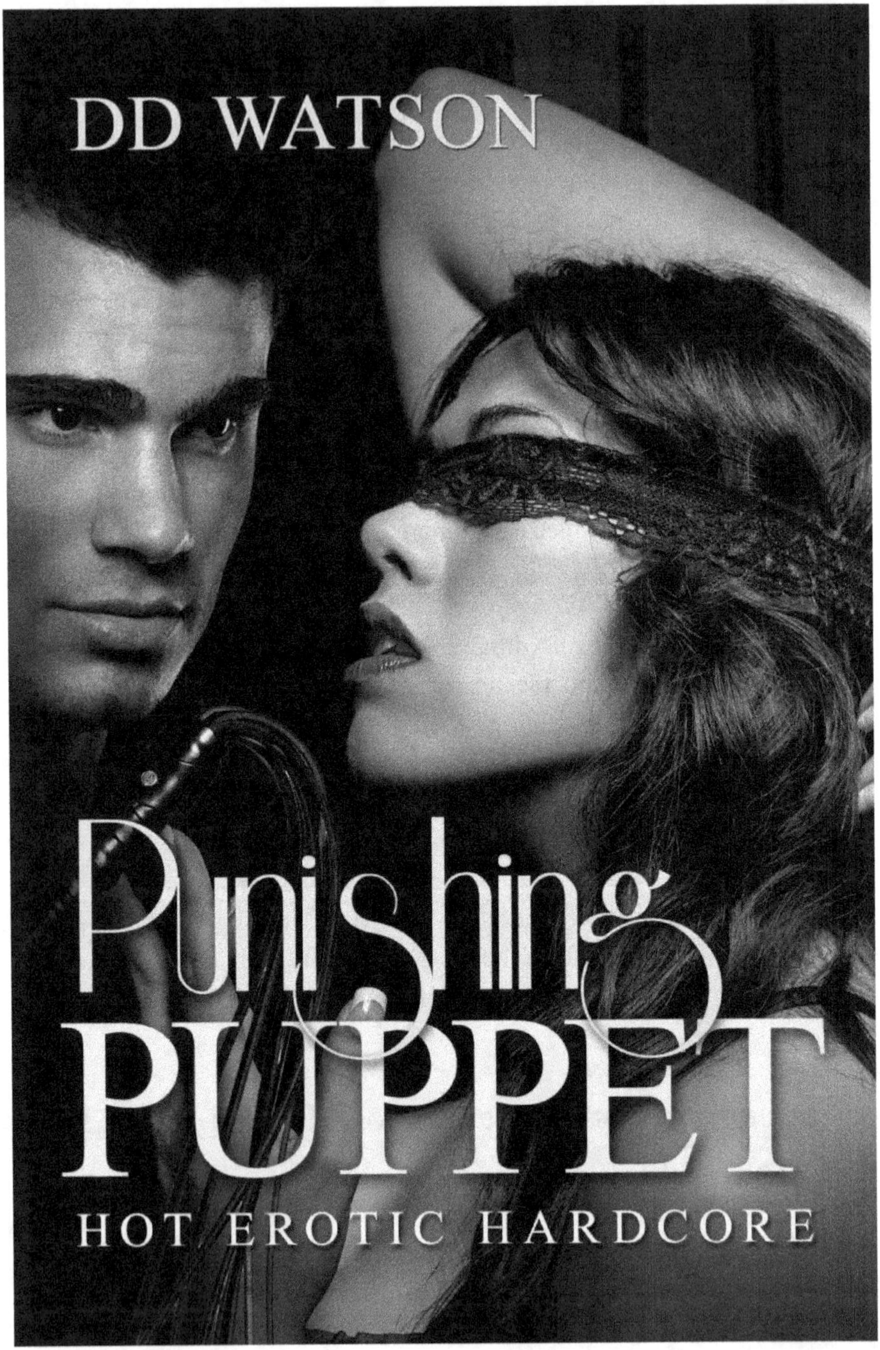
DD WATSON
Punishing
PUPPET
HOT EROTIC HARDCORE

Her head floated from side to side as she willed her eyes open. Her eyelashes parted to allow light in, but there was only darkness. The drug injected into her held her still even though her legs and arms were free.

She began to remember how she came to be where she was. The ride in the car trunk was by far bouncy but warm. When the trunk was open, her Master was there but didn't assist her out of it only his driver and another male she didn't recognize hauled her out. Before she could assess where she was the driver placed a patch on her neck, and her world went black again.

Puppet was never one to dwell on any negative situation. She trusted her Master Troy, no matter how mad he was with her breaking his rules he loved her unconditionally.

Going to the island was a set punishment but Puppet saw it as a learning experience. One she plans on succeeding in to make her Master proud.

She took in a deep breath and slowly exhaled it. That seem to help because she was able to move her fingers and toes sending a tingling sensation through her arms and legs. Puppet felt a growing chuckle inside her as if she was being tickled under her skin.

A smile spread on her cheeks as she tried to remain still to avoid another attack.

"You're awake," said the voice of a male that sat on the floor right beside her.

"Yes," she moaned. "You can see me?"

"Well yeah."

"So—it's not dark in here?"

"No it's very well lit you're just wearing a blindfold and the drug given to you is slowly wearing off."

"Oh, so where is the light coming from?"

"Window with a view of the garden showing a lovely sunny day."

"Why aren't you wearing a blindfold?"

"Because I'm here to watch you."

"Oh, so I'm on the island?"

"That is correct."

"Where's my Master Troy?"

"I'm not at liberty to say Puppet."

"And you know me. Am I allowed to be asking you questions?"

"With permission."

"By you?"

"No, by my Master—Shawn," he said, glancing up at the green eyed male who handpicked him out of a dozen. Took ownership, making him his personal pet; he stood clean shaven wearing black jeans, biker boots and shirtless. His long black mane hung loose on his shoulders. Two men stood behind him both wearing leather pants black boots and chest harnesses with buzz cut hairstyles.

"Is Master Shawn training me because I disappointed my Master?"

"He is."

"Is he listening to us?"

"Yes."

"Is he here in the room with us?"

He was signaled to silence by Shawn hovering his fingers in front of his pet's mouth. Shawn sat beside Puppet and leaned into her ear.

"I'm right here Puppet." His accent vibrated through her ears as she took in the heavenly scent that radiated from his skin.

Puppet enjoyed the tender time she was allowed to spend with him even though she hasn't laid eyes on him yet.

"That will be all Peter you may return to your duties."

"Thank you Master." On hand and knee Peter crawled out of the room followed by one of the males. Turning his attention back to Puppet, Shawn took his fingers and traveled over her naked skin, igniting the sensation that tortured her a moment ago.

Puppet tried to keep a straight face but regaining some movement in his limbs she began to squirm and giggle. Shawn only watched as she didn't try to push him away but seem to enjoy the torment. He watched her nipples harden as he flicked them with two fingers. Then running them between her legs he felt the wetness building in the soft folds of her crouch. He brought his drenched fingers to her mouth and pressed them pass her lips where she sucked and licked them clean. He removed them and rose to his feet.

"Get her to her knees on the floor and face her to the bed," he ordered a male who moved quickly to perform his task. Jerking Puppet up, he forced her into position as Shawn instructed.

Shawn walked over to a duffle bag opened in the corner and removed a handheld whip. The handle was as long as his arm with nine tails all knotted. When he returned his attention to Puppet, still blindfolded on her knees, he didn't hesitate. When the first strike landed she let out a deep cry that ricocheted around them. He landed another that resulted in the same. He picked up the tempo and continued to strike her back and arse until the welts glowed a profound red.

"How many blows did I give you Puppet?" He asked watching her claw at the mattress. "Answer me," he snapped striking her again.

"Six—teen—Master."

"Splendid, most pets never count. Troy has been training you."

"Yes Master—my Master is good to his pet."

"A little too good, or you wouldn't be here Puppet."

"Yes Master."

He switched the whip in his opposite hand and walked over to Puppet, snatching the blindfold from her eyes.

"Turn around Puppet and place your arms on the bed for support but remain on your knees."

"Yes Master." She turned clumsily but managed, getting her first glimpse of the notorious Shawn. The man whom her Master said strikes fear in any pet who crosses his path. Why was she not afraid? Was he just playing with her? She caught his emerald eyes, which shot ice daggers at her. His chiseled looks could rival her Master Troy's.

"Troy mentioned you were hard-headed. Who said you could look at my eyes?"

Puppet caught on, but it was too late as he began to whip her chest, stomach and thighs. The pain was more intense, but she kept her arm on the bed and didn't try to run away. Her Master Troy whipped her in this same manner on different occasions, so she grew to accept her punishments no matter how unforgiving they were.

When he stopped, she collapsed onto the floor at his feet breathing intensely but not unconscious.

"Take her to the groomers and tell them I'll call when I'm ready for her."

The male lifted Puppet up as if she didn't weigh a thing and draped her on his shoulder carrying her out of the room.

Peter had lied to Puppet, who was hanging upside down. She glanced around the room and saw no window only a ceiling light, mirrors and two doors.

Once Puppet was gone the second door opened, and Troy walked in wearing his full business attire. Shawn turned and smiled at his old friend from school whose dreams mimicked his.

"So what's your conclusion?" asked Troy.

"She's knows what she wants. I never saw a first timer take what she took from me. Or—maybe I've become soft."

"No, it's not you, Puppet is without doubt atypical. I can do anything to her, anything I wish."

"Then why bring her to me? Apparently you have a handle on her."

"No, she's become hesitant and explorative, not asking permission."

"She's evolving?"

"It has been five years. And as I said she'd taken my treatments without complaint."

"Do you want me to train her to be a dominatrix?"

Troy fell silent as he glanced to the floor. He closed his eyes and remembered his devoted pet and how she found him. Shawn's strong hand rested on his friend's shoulder waking him from his thoughts.

"It's been a long trip for you both, come and relax with me and let the groomer spoil her. A good meal, drink and sucking will clear your mind to make a decision."

That brought a grin to Troy's face as he let Shawn lead him out of the room.


If you enjoyed this sample then look for **Punishing Puppet**.

# SAVING
## Heather

**HOT ROMANCE EROTICA**
# LILITH JONES

She went into his arms. Her kiss had been intended to be a light acceptance of his niceness. He kept it up, though, and she certainly had no reason to end it. He sucked her lower lip, and then he licked her lips. She opened them to him, but he kept licking them. She finally sought his tongue with hers. When they met, sparks flew. He pulled her to him, and she felt his firmness against her stomach.

"Oh, my love," he said when they broke. His hands went to the buttons on her blouse. She was his, and she let him strip her. He did it slowly, kissing every newly revealed inch of skin. She felt aroused, more aroused than she had been in years. She also felt cherished, cherished as not even the Rick of years ago had cherished her.

When he was kneeling and he had her jeans down around her ankles, he eased back to let her step out of them. Then he kissed her legs upward to her panties. He kissed her mound through those panties, and she felt ready for him. He eased her down on the bed.

If he'd been patience personified in removing her clothes, he was nearly a blur in removing his. Then he faced her, fully nude and magnificently male. He looked as ready for her as she felt ready for him. She pushed the panties down, and Rick took them off her feet. She spread her legs slightly as he got into bed.

He started with a kiss, though. It was a gentle, but extremely sensual, kiss. She arched her hips off the bed as their tongues met. He cupped her, holding all her femininity. As he moved his mouth from hers to her breasts, her nipple strained upward towards his mouth. He licked it, touching only the tip with the tip of his tongue. She quivered all over, and he moved to the other breast. When he sucked that nipple, sparks shot from the tips of her toes.

He thrust one finger deep inside her. Then he drew it out, very slowly, and over her clit. It was only one finger, but it went so slowly that it felt much more -- maybe a yard long. He changed breasts again and sucked deeply. The sucking and the stroking were sending heat through her. She felt as though she was being baked, and there was a fire in her womb.

He raised his head from her breast and stared into her eyes. "Heather," he said. "Heather, my love."

Then lightning crackled within her. She moaned and writhed. It went on as he kept stroking. She collapsed, and he removed his finger. He kissed her forehead and her shoulder. As her breath eased, he kissed her nose tip, and then her breasts, and then her stomach.

He again stroked her mound. He rubbed the lips there against one another, very softly. The response, however, was fire. His hand was wonderful, and his look was loving if it was searching. He had brought her delight, and she could believe he would bring her more delight. She wanted more than that, though.

"You," she said. "Please!" He rolled away suddenly. She stifled a protest when she saw that he was reaching in his drawer. She almost told him that he didn't need the rubber. She could tell, though, that this was one more act of caring. He was taking responsibility, taking care of her. Whatever the physical shortcomings, she would celebrate it as an action of the man who would never put her at risk.

Now, he was kneeling between her legs. She spread her lips with her hand and rolled her hips to receive him fully. She felt open to him.

"Heather," he said.

"Yes, oh yes."

However open she had been, she felt him stretch her more as he went in slowly. And it was slow, agonizingly slow. When he had filled her, he kissed her briefly. She hugged him with her arms and with her legs. He was in her, but she wanted to hold all of him.

He withdrew as slowly, and he felt a need for him to return. He thrust in a little faster, and she felt herself burn. As he sped up, it was never fast enough. She thrust up to engulf him as he came down. Then the lightning crashed through her again.

He withdrew half way, rammed into her, and pulsed deep within her. For a second, he was one rigid arch within her hug. Then he collapsed onto his elbows. She, too, relaxed. Her feet rested on his calves, and her hands rested on his back, but she was no longer really hugging him.

That was closeness. They were one. She was disappointed when he moved away, although the freedom to breathe was a relief. He moved off the bed and turned off the overhead light. As he came back, she heard the rubber drop into the wastebasket.

"We really need another pillow," he said as he got into bed. He lay down beside her and pulled her into a hug. He carefully spread the sheet over both of them.

"We don't really need a wider bed, though," she said. He chuckled. "Y'know . . . Maybe you don't know. I'm on the pill."

"Well, it didn't seem a good time to ask."

"It wasn't. You took care of me."

"I always will," he said. "Somebody should. You work too hard taking care of Anne. Somebody has to take care of you."

"Well, maybe, we'll take care of each other."

"That's a good idea. I love you. Seriously, if we're going to be a family, we'll have to divide up the family tasks. Probably, you should do the dividing. But give me some of the tasks of caring for Anne. Just because I don't know how, doesn't mean I can't learn."

"You do great. I might have to give her the baths and wash her clothes, but you give her kisses and protect her."

"Washing her clothes and yours can't be all that different from washing mine, and I wash mine already. Anyway, first you get the divorce, preferably with full custody. Next we get married. Then, if I can, I adopt her. After that, we'll try to get her to call me Daddy."

"I love you." Heather thought Rick's project to get Anne to call him Daddy reflected more of the story that she'd heard at the funeral than Anne's situation. Right now, Anne had two men in her life. One beat her, and she called him Daddy. The other hugged her, and she called him Rick. Anne would know which name meant love. Well, courts took forever, and four-year-olds were resilient. By the time Rick had gone through his agenda, Anne would call him anything he wanted.

"And I love you, too," Rick said. She believed him. His hand stroked up to her breast, and she patted it and held it there. "Is this what married people do?" he asked. "I mean lie in bed and talk later?"

"Well, I'm not sure that I want my last marriage to be a model." And that was an understatement. Too many of her conversations with Bill had been at the top of their lungs. "Is this what you want our marriage to be?"

"Yeah. Especially this part." He squeezed her breast very lightly. "I like holding you."

"And," she said in satisfaction, "I like being held by you."

If you enjoyed this sample then look for **Saving Heather**.

# WANT FREE COPIES OF MY BOOKS?

Just visit my blog and download free copies of my books:

**awesomeauthors.org/justplainbob**